The Geezer Bench
Scott Fields

Cover Art:
Michelle Crocker
www.mlcdesigns4you.com

Publisher's Note:

This is a work of fiction. All names, characters, places, and events are the work of the author's imagination.

Any resemblance to real persons, places, or events is coincidental.

Solstice Publishing - www.solsticepublishing.com

# The Geezer Bench

## By Scott Fields

Scott Fields

## Chapter One

It was the first day of spring, or at least that's what the calendar said. The only remaining remnants of winter were the dark gray piles of snow that dotted the roadsides. Life was slowly returning to the small farming community. It was still cold, but the robins were back, and the crocuses were emerging from the ground. The days were getting longer, and the promise of warm days was in the air.

Just outside of town, a small white farmhouse and its pristine white outbuildings stood proudly on a small hill. Vast snow-covered fields lay dormant from the long cold winter. It was certain that they would soon be awakening from a long winter's sleep.

Murphy opened the closet and pulled out a dark weathered coat. He slipped it on and started for the backdoor.

An old woman nearly ran across the room. "Where are you going, you old fool?" she asked.

"Where do you think I'm going, Kat?" he asked. "It's the first day of spring."

"It's too cold for you to sit out there on that on that old park bench with those friends of yours."

"I've been going out there for the last ten years, and I'm not stopping now," he said zipping up his coat.

"It's too cold, I'm telling you," she said, straightening his collar. "You know darn well the other three won't be there."

"Well, I'm pretty sure Jed won't, since he went and died last December."

"Land's sakes, you are one stubborn old man," she said, shaking a finger at him.

The old man opened the backdoor. "I won't be long," he said and walked out the door.

"Don't come crying to me when you catch a cold," shouted Katherine.

Murphy raised one hand as he walked away.

La Rue was a small farming community nestled alongside the Scioto River. With less than a thousand residents and little or no industry, it relied heavily on the income of the surrounding farms. The downtown business district was only three blocks of businesses on both sides of the street. In spite of its small size, the town boasted of four grocery stores, two hardware stores, four gas stations and two elevators for processing the farmers' yields.

Murphy turned down High Street and parked in front of Lingo's Dry Goods Store. Near the front door and backed up against the wall were two park benches nearly four feet in length. The paint was peeling and they were badly in need of repair, but over the years they had served as home away from home for a very select group of men. To belong, the rules were simple. There were only four members permitted, one had to be at least sixty-five and retired, and he needed the approval of all of the other members.

"Where the hell have you been, Murphy?" asked Walter getting to his feet.

Murphy slid out of his truck and closed the door behind him. "Hi to you too, Walt," he said. He turned to the other man still sitting on the bench. "I thought things might be different this year, but I see he's still cranky as ever."

"Well, excuse me," said Walter. "I was worried about you. You're always the first one here."

Murphy stepped over to the other man sitting on the bench. He had his arms wrapped around himself and was shaking violently. "Good morning, Sully," said Murphy. "You look as if you're a bit cold."

"I have a very low tolerance for the cold," said Sully.

Walter turned in his direction. "You have a very low tolerance for the heat as well."

"I think it has something to do with my metabolism," said Sully.

"I think it has something to do with the fact that you're a faggot," said Walter.

Murphy took a seat on the other bench. "Well, I see nothing has changed."

"That's for sure," said Walter. "He's still gay, and he's still living with me."

"Just because I'm not as crude and barbaric as you, doesn't mean I'm gay," said Sully. "I have a refinement that you wouldn't understand."

Murphy slowly shook his head. "You two are picking up where you left off last fall."

"Murphy, it never stops," said Walter. "I put up with this butt-lickin' moron everyday. Oh, I'm sorry, this butt-lickin' *refined* moron."

Sully sat straight up. "The only reason I don't stand up and hit you is…is…"

"Is because I'll beat you to a pulp," said Walter.

Murphy turned to the others. "I think I found a replacement for Jed."

"Isn't it a bit too soon?" muttered Sully.

"He's been dead for over three months," said Walter. "Who did you find?"

"Riley Hoagland," blurted Murphy.

"Riley Hoagland?" shouted Walter. "He's not even old enough, is he?"

"He'll be sixty-five next month."

"Wow," muttered Walter. "Doesn't look it."

"I think Riley is an excellent choice," said Sully.

"No one asked you, Sparky," said Walter.

"Well, as a matter of fact, we all must be in agreement," said Murphy. "We don't have many rules, but that's one of them."

"We might have to make up one more rule," said Walter with a smile. "We might have to choose someone who can fit on one of these benches."

"He'll be fine," said Murphy. "There's room for four of us."

Walter studied the two benches. "I don't know. His ass is big enough for a license plate."

"That's disgusting," said Sully.

"I heard that he has his own zip code," said Walter.

"Well, I can see where this is heading," said Murphy.

"No, no," said Walter. "I vote that we bring him on board."

Murphy turned with a puzzled look. "Why the change of heart?"

"Jed was too straight-laced," said Walter. "At least with Riley, I've got something to make fun of."

"You are such a pig," muttered Sully.

"When is he coming?" asked Walter.

"I told him to stop by tomorrow," said Murphy. "I wanted to see what you two thought first."

"He's never been married, has he?" asked Walter with a smirk.

"I don't think so," said Murphy.

There was a pause.

"He's still living with his mother, isn't he?"

Murphy turned and stared at Walter. "Yes, and she's eighty-five years old. I know where you're going with this, Walter."

"I say bring him on," said Walter spreading his arms in the air. "Things have been rather boring around here."

There was a pause, and then Sully leaned forward. "I can't believe we're having this conversation. It shows no respect for Jed."

"I disagree," said Walter. "Jed would have got a laugh out of this whole thing. He always said that he gauged how good of a day he had by the number of times he laughed."

"Now, Walter, I know we make fun of each other, but this guy is different," said Murphy. "You could really hurt his feelings if you get started on his weight. If you're going there, tell me now and I'll call the whole thing off."

"Jesus, Murphy," said Walter. "What's got your panties in a bunch?"

"What if someone was to make fun of your bald head or your incredibly low IQ?" Sully asked.

"Fat people don't need for someone to tell them they're fat," said Murphy. "They already know it."

"Alright, for Christ's sakes," said Walter. "I'll leave him alone. Sure is going to be boring around here."

"Has anybody else asked about joining?" asked Murphy.

"Nobody with any self-respect," said Walter.

"Well, I'll call Riley tonight and warn him," said Murphy. "If he's still interested, we might see him tomorrow."

There was a pause as if to say that was the end of that issue.

"How's Kat doing?" asked Sully.

"Oh, she has her good days and her bad," said Murphy.

"Did she ever decide to get that chemotherapy?" asked Walter.

"She tells me the only thing she has left is her hair, and she ain't giving it up," said Murphy. He paused for a moment staring at the back of his weathered hands. "It's too late for her anyhow. Doc says it would only give her maybe a month."

"Seems to me an extra month would be worth quite a bit," said Walter with an unusually quiet voice.

"She wants to live her last days with dignity," said Murphy bowing his head. "And if ever there was a decision that is hers and hers alone to make, it's that one."

Nobody said anything for the next several moments.

"Sorry, Murphy," muttered Walter.

"So, what have you been up to, Walter?" Murphy asked. "I haven't seen you in quite some time."

Walter smiled. "I took Agnes Dutton out on a date a couple weeks ago."

"Well, what do you know about that?" said Murphy.

By that time, Walter was beaming with pride. "Yes, siree. Ole Walt's still got it."

"Where did you take her?" asked Murphy.

"The American Legion was having their monthly fish fry," said Walter. "I've tasted better, but you always walk away with a full stomach."

Sully laughed. "You sure know how to show a woman a good time."

"What are you laughing at?" said Walter. "Agnes had seconds."

Sully laughed again. "Has she gone out with you since?"

"Agnes is a busy woman," said Walter. "She can't just break away when she wants to."

"She's the librarian," said Sully. "And the library is only open three days a week."

Murphy turned to Walter. "You know Agnes is a distant relative of mine. I hope you treated her with respect."

"Nothing but," said Walter. "I didn't even kiss her good night."

"Lucky thing for her," said Sully with a smirk. "They tell me that hoof-and-mouth disease is hard to shake."

Walter turned and stared at Sully. "You'd better get started."

"Started at what?" asked Sully.

"Walking home, because you ain't riding with me."

"So, what do you think, Walt?" asked Murphy. "Is Agnes the one?"

"Not sure yet," said Walter. "She makes a great potato salad, and that's important with me. You know there are only two kinds of potato salads…good and bad."

"Well, it's important that she measures up," said Murphy.

"We're going out again," Walter announced.

"Where are you taking her this time?" asked Sully. "Are you taking her on a cruise or just a plane ride?"

"I thought I'd take her bowling," said Walter.

"Bowling," said Murphy. "Agnes has a bad hip. She's had it for over ten years now. She doesn't like to call it what it really is, but I'm almost sure she has bursitis."

"You don't take a woman on a date and take her bowling anyhow," said Sully. "You need to take her to some elegant restaurant with French cuisine and an orchestra playing soft music for dancing."

"Oh, I plan to take her to the diner afterwards. You know how good the burgers are there. We might even split an order of fries."

"Oh, good Lord," muttered Sully.

"And then, if we decide to show each other some moves, they've got a jukebox in that place," said Walter. "Don't see many of those anymore."

"You don't see many like you anymore either," muttered Sully.

Murphy cleared his throat and turned to Sully. "What about you, Sully? I thought I heard that you were getting back together with Margot."

"We met for lunch at that horrid diner about a month ago," said Sully.

"Well, that's a start," said Murphy.

"We met to discuss the only thing we still have in common, or for that matter, ever had in common; our son, Simon," said Sully. "This wasn't a romantic meeting as those disgusting thugs who sit in there all day long eating and drinking swill would suggest."

"Fred Johnson had you practically kneeling at the altar again," said Murphy.

"Fred Johnson eats his own boogers," said Sully. "I've seen him do it countless times. How trustworthy could such a vile creature be? Of course, I must confess that it couldn't be any less tasty or, for that matter, less nutritious than the special of the day."

"Is your son okay?" asked Murphy.

"Oh, by all means. He just wants to borrow some money. Margot was good enough to pass that particular problem onto me."

"How you ever sired a child is beyond me," muttered Walter.

"Obviously, I don't have any money to spare," said Scully. "If I did, I wouldn't be living in the squalor that I'm living in today."

"Squalor!" shouted Walter. "You know, you're free to leave anytime…"

Murphy slowly got to his feet. He stretched his stiff back and stood straight. "I hate putting an end to this stimulating conversation, but I need to go home."

"Anything wrong?" asked Sully.

"I don't know," muttered Murphy. "I just need to check on Kat."

"Give her our best," said Sully.

Theirs was a good marriage, this union between Murphy and Katherine. Spanning nearly fifty years, they spent their lives embraced in love and devotion to one another. For all of his life, Murphy had farmed sixty acres and had managed to support Katherine and their two sons. Having reached retirement years before, both Murphy and

Katherine decided that they would spend their few remaining years in the comfort of their own home.

Then it happened. The doctor blurted the word with such callous ease. This union of good times and bad, of tears and laughter and of success and failure was coming to an end. The light in her eyes would soon be dimmed and forever stolen from Murphy's life. As if in defiance, Murphy went about his daily life as if the word, "cancer" had never been spoken. He saw it in her eyes. She had relied on him, counted on him for all these years, and now she looked to him for help, the kind of help he could not give. She saw it in his eyes. He had been there for her, doing his best to help her for so many years, and now stared, helplessly, into her eyes yearning for answers that would never be.

How could God take this woman from him? It was if his very heart and soul were about to be ripped from his body. Why did he fall in love with this woman? Why did he marry her, raise children with her? Why did he spend all these years loving this wonderful woman just to have her taken from him. It didn't seem fair.

The near and distant future alike seemed so cold and uncertain. Who would share his good times and heal the bad? Who would laugh with him and cry when he was sad? Gone would be this woman of unconditional love and gentle caring. Never again would he find warmth and comfort from those loving eyes. It was as if life was about to wrap a bitterly cold blanket around him. Indeed, it just didn't seem fair.

Murphy opened the backdoor and closed it behind him. He scanned the kitchen and there was nobody there. That seemed strange to him. Katherine spent most of her day in the kitchen fixing one thing or another. He hung up his coat and hat and stepped into the living room. "Kat," he called out.

"I'm in here," she replied from the bedroom.

Murphy opened the door and found her lying in bed. "Are you okay?" he asked.

"Oh, I'm fine," she said forcing a smile. "I just felt a little dizzy."

Murphy sat in a chair next to her. "Are you sure?" he asked. "I don't think I ever saw you in bed this time of day."

"It doesn't hurt to squeeze in a nap every once in awhile," she said stretching out in the bed.

There was a long pause as Murphy sat motionless staring aimlessly at the wall. After several moments, his eyes began to glisten and a lone tear streaked down the side of his face.

"What's the matter?" asked Katherine thrusting her hand in his direction.

He scooted his chair closer and took her hand in his burying it with his other hand. As he leaned forward, the tears flowed. "I don't want to lose you," he said trying to compose himself.

Katherine sat up in bed. "I know, Murphy."

"We've been together for so long, I don't even know what life would be like without you," he said.

Katherine swung her feet out of bed and wrapped her arms around this man who had loved and protected her for so many years.

Murphy leaned back and took a deep breath. "I'm so sorry, Kat," he said wiping his eyes. "You've got enough to worry about without my breaking down in front of you."

"It's okay," she said, forcing a smile meant to reassure him.

"Dear God, the years went fast," he said glancing at the ceiling. "Seems like only yesterday when we were going out on our first date."

"Do you remember that you picked me up in your father's truck?"

"We were darn lucky to have that," said Murphy with the hint of a smile. "I don't know whether you ever knew this, but, at first, he was only going to let me use the tractor. Can you imagine? There probably wouldn't have been a second date if I had picked you up in a tractor."

"Where in the world would I have ridden? As I recall, there's only one seat on a tractor."

Murphy scratched his head. "I guess you would have had to sit on my lap."

Katherine laughed. "We both know better than that. You were the shiest boy in our class. There's no way you would have ever suggested such a thing."

Murphy smiled. "Yeah, I suppose you're right. Thank God Pop let me use the truck. You might never have married me."

"Oh, I don't know," she said playfully. "I was pretty smitten with you. Actually, I had my eye on you back in the first grade. Oh, you didn't even know I existed. You were more interested in sports and guy stuff."

Murphy turned to her. "Well, I don't remember you saying anything or giving me the impression that you cared."

"Oh, Murphy, you were too busy playing games with the other boys. I'll bet you didn't even notice that in every class picture from first grade on up, I'm right next to you."

"Why would I think anything about…?"

"Don't you remember?" she asked. "We were supposed to line up alphabetically. Harden is really close to Flemming, but unfortunately for me Don Kramer just happened to be in every one of our classes. Every year it cost me a bagful of cookies to get Don to trade places with me."

"You bribed him with cookies?"

"Every year."

"You got off easy."

"Why do you say that?"

"Don became the biggest skinflint in the county. They say he has the first dollar he ever earned."

There was a long pause.

The smile disappeared from Murphy's face. "I'm sorry, Kat," he said. "You look to me for strength, and here I am blubbering like a kid in school."

"My goodness, Murphy, I would think most anybody would at least shed a tear under the circumstances," she said as she swung her feet out of bed.

"What are you doing?" asked Murphy.

"I'm getting up," she said with a smile. "I feel fine."

"Why don't you take the day off and stay in bed?"

"I have too much work to do," she said getting to her feet. "Besides, I feel just fine."

"You sure are one stubborn woman," he said getting up and putting his arm around her. "I know I don't say it often enough, but I do love you, Mrs. Flemming."

"And I love you, Mr. Flemming," she said kissing him on the cheek. "Now move out of the way, so that I can get to work."

# Chapter Two

Riley Hoagland tucked the shirttails of his new shirt in his jeans and stared into the mirror. He had been overweight his whole life, and had, in fact, been on and off diets since he was a child. When he was sixteen, his mother saved enough money to take Riley to the doctor to see if there was anything that could be done. He offered no medication nor did he even mention diet or exercise. He simply informed them that Riley was born that way and that there was nothing neither he nor anybody could do about it. For that bit of information, Mrs. Hoagland handed over the wad of bills that she had so frugally saved.

Riley picked up a bottle of cologne and dabbed a drop or two on his neck. “Unfortunately, it doesn’t get any better than this,” he muttered into the mirror, turned, and walked away.

Riley had lived with his mother all of his life. She was a kind, church-going woman and highly-respected by all who knew her, but, unfortunately, for Riley, she was a very possessive and controlling woman as well. Riley’s father endured her for over twelve years, and then one day walked out of the house and never returned. Everyone in town knew why he left. It was the subject of gossip for months. Such trite conversations were neither a bother nor a concern for her, but it became regarded by Riley as his most humiliating experience.

Besides being a controlling type person, Thelma Hoagland was also a hypochondriac. It was common knowledge that for every sickness that was prevalent in town, Thelma was not only stricken with it, but had two other maladies as well. To that end, nearly all her time was spent in bed, not only to aid her recovery but to avoid the afflicted who might spread contaminating germs to her.

"I'm leaving now, Mother," he said putting on his coat.

Thelma sat up in bed. "I wish you wouldn't go down there," she said her voice cracking. "You're just asking for more heartache."

"It isn't the same, Mother. They invited me to sit with them."

"We both know why, don't we?"

"Yeah, I do," said Riley. "They want me to join them in an hour of friendship and idle talk."

"What makes you think they'll be any different from the others?"

"These are good men, Mother," he said, his voice a bit louder. "They are old men, and old men don't act like that."

"Do you remember your sixteenth birthday party? That's what you can expect, Riley. Nothing changes. People are basically mean through and through. You mark my words. You are heading for nothing but a heartache. Isn't that Sullivan Baker a part of those delinquents?"

"Now, don't start on him," said Riley with a determined voice.

"Why on earth would they ever invite a homosexual is beyond me. You just be careful around him. He has to be a bad influence."

"Sully is a good man. Besides that, it has never been proven if he is gay or not."

"For God's sakes, Riley," she said. "You don't need a judge and jury for that one. Just look at the man, and if that doesn't convince you, listen to him speak."

Riley walked across the room and stood in the open doorway to his mother's bedroom. "You know, Mother, sometimes I can't believe you have the nerve to call yourself a Christian."

"Don't start with me," she said rising even further out of bed. "God doesn't like queers anymore than I do."

"And just how would you know what God likes and doesn't like?"

"Says so in the Bible."

"So, you're telling me that somewhere in the Bible, God said that he hates homosexuals."

"Don't be flippant," she said. "You're talking about God stuff now."

"Look to yourself, Mother." You're accusing God of hating a group of people. I'm not so sure He would approve."

"Shame on you, Riley Hoagland. You shouldn't..."

Riley turned and headed for the backdoor. "Gotta go, Mother. See you later."

***

Murphy stepped out of his truck and closed the door. He glanced over to the sidewalk to find one of the benches already occupied.

"Good morning, gentlemen," said Murphy as he stepped on the curb.

"You're late again, Murphy," said Walter leaning back on the bench. "What seems to have captured your attention?"

"Kat," he muttered and paused until he was seated. "She tells me she's okay, but I know differently."

"Is she in any pain?" Walter asked.

"If she is, she's keeping it from me."

"She's a good woman, Murphy," said Walter. "She doesn't deserve this. I still say God won't take her just yet. The world needs people like her right now."

Murphy ran his fingers through his hair. "Well, I hope you're right."

"On a brighter note," said Walter. "Did you contact Riley?"

"I sure did," said Murphy.

"Is he coming?" asked Walter with a smile.

"I believe he is."

Walter rubbed his hands together with excitement. "That's fantastic."

"You're such a pig," said Sully, turning away from Walter.

"There you go again with that name calling," said Walter. "In the first place, I've known Riley a hell of a lot longer than you, and in the second place, I have no intention of hurting his feelings. Actually, I've always thought that there are people who were destined to be fat no matter what they do. It's just the way they are."

"Well, that's a relief," muttered Sully.

"It's just like you," said Walter. "You can't help it that you want to stick your tongue down a man's throat. It's just the way you are."

"God, I hate you," said Sully, crossing his legs.

"Can't say we discriminate," said Walter. "We got a fat guy and a queer. All we need is a black guy, and we're politically correct."

"Those are two words that have been the downfall of our country," said Murphy.

"What two words are those?" asked Riley, standing beside them.

The three men jumped and turned.

"How long have you been standing there?" asked Murphy.

"Long enough to wonder if I'm the fat guy or the queer," said Riley.

"Oops," said Walter.

"May I sit down?" he asked.

"Help yourself," said Murphy.

"You're a brave man, Murphy, to invite me to park my fat ass beside you on that rickety bench," said Riley. He eased himself down next to Murphy. "They don't build them like they used to."

"You know the others, don't you?" asked Murphy.

"Yeah, sure. Mornin', Walt…Sully."

"We were talking about how the term, 'politically correct' has been the downfall of our country," said Murphy.

"Oh, I don't know," said Riley. "There are many changes happening in our society right now that are long overdue. The white male has dominated the world for so long and now we're seeing women and minorities taking the reins. I view that as a positive change that would be considered politically correct."

Walter slowly shook his head. "Sweet Jesus, we have a liberal."

Murphy held up his hand to Walter. "Now hang on, Walt. Let's give him a chance. He has a right to his opinion."

"Yeah, but his opinion sucks."

"Walter, let the man speak," said Sully. "It's about time we had someone with normal, today kind of thinking."

"Go ahead," said Murphy. "Speak your thoughts."

"Well, I don't have much else to say," said Riley. "I just think it's time we let others be in charge."

Murphy leaned forward. "Do you think we should promote women and minorities over white men at any expense?"

"I don't understand," said Riley.

"For years and years, policemen have been taking a test to get promoted. To satisfy the judicial system in this country that is quite frankly monitoring the promotion of women and minorities, scores are ignored on this test. Since white men generally score higher, they simply ignore the scores and promote everyone but white men. In some cities, they're getting in trouble by doing this, so they now have a test for white men and one for everyone else. As you might guess, white men now score much lower because of how much more difficult their tests are. Do you think that this falls under the heading of politically correct?"

"Well, I suppose the goal of..."

"You don't understand, Mr. Hoagland," said Murphy. "Our judicial system is enforcing this all across the country. We have women working in jobs that are difficult even for strong men. My nephew works for a demolition company. He works all day long hauling brick, mortar and steel by hand while women making the same wages sit and watch them. At the end of the day, the women spend a half hour sweeping up after them. Does that sound politically correct to you?"

Walter laughed aloud. "Murphy, I've never seen you like this. We should have recruited a liberal a long time ago."

Murphy leaned back. "I suppose you're right. I'm sorry."

"Don't apologize, Murphy," said Walter. "You're on a roll."

"I know I shouldn't let things like that bother me, but there are so many people making decisions and judgments based on the seven o'clock news. Everyone is slapping each other on the back for doing what is politically correct, and yet they haven't a clue as to what's really going on. They hire a woman into a man's job and are satisfied they did the right thing. What they don't know is she can't do the work, and men now have to do their work as well as hers."

"Go, Murphy, go," said Walter.

There was a pause.

"May I ask where you get this information?" asked Riley.

"Right from the trenches, Riley," said Murphy. "I don't believe a thing I read in the papers or see on TV. I believe my friends and relatives and trust them to tell me the truth."

"Well, we certainly laid out the welcome mat for our new member," said Sully.

Murphy jumped to his feet. “Oh, good Lord. You’re right, Sully. Talk about bad manners,” he said and extended his hand.

Riley shook his hand and said, “Don’t worry about it. I enjoy a good healthy debate from time to time. I guess I’m not prepared for today’s subject matter. I’ll pass for today.”

“Oh, please don’t back down,” said Sully. “These Neanderthals need someone to stand up to them. They seriously believe that they have all the answers.”

“Trust me, Sully,” said Walter. “If I had any brains, I would have figured out how to get rid of you years ago.”

“Let’s start over,” said Murphy easing himself back down on the bench. “It just seems like things got all messed up today. Let’s do it right now.”

“I don’t know,” said Walter. “It seemed normal to me.”

“Riley, tell us about yourself,” said Murphy. “And Walter, you be quiet.”

Everyone leaned forward as if waiting to hear juicy details.

“Sorry to disappoint you guys, but there’s not much to tell,” said Riley. “I live with my mother and always have.” He paused. “Jesus, I’ve never said that out loud. That sounds disturbing. Or disturbed.”

“Have you ever been married?” asked Murphy.

“Can’t say as I have.”

“Any girlfriends?” asked Walter.

Riley leaned back and pointed at his stomach with both fingers. “Do you really think that a woman would go out with me? Seems like I’ve been on a diet all my life. I’ll lose twenty pounds, and the next thing you know there’s a birthday party for a friend and we’re all meeting at the buffet. Guess what? I end up finding that twenty pounds I had lost.”

"So what you're telling us is you've never been out on a date," said Walter with a trace of a smile. "Is that right?"

Riley slowly shook his head.

"Are you telling us that you are a virgin?" asked Walter.

Riley stared at Walter for several moments with a disgusted look on his face. "That's exactly what I'm telling you," he said.

"You're a sixty-five year old virgin?" asked Walter not really expecting a reply.

"Actually, I'm sixty-four. I don't really turn…"

"Dear Lord, we gotta get this man laid," shouted Walter. "No man should go to his grave without experiencing the rapture and exaltation of having sex with a woman."

"Good God, Walter!" said Riley looking right and left. "Can you hold it down a bit?"

"I'm not talking about sex with one of your farm animals," said Walter. "I'm talking in-the-bed, dirty, sweaty, hallelujah, makin' love with a woman kind of sex, and I can fix you up with a woman who doesn't care what you look like as long as you have fifty bucks on you."

"Now, never mind," said Riley. "I've got my eye on someone."

"Who is this dreamboat?" asked Walter.

"Well, I don't want to tell you. You might tip her off."

"Have you asked this girl out yet?"

"No."

"Why not?"

"I want to lose some weight first."

"She must be really something if you want to lose weight," said Walter. "Come on. What's her name?"

"It's Clara Butts," mumbled Riley.

Murphy leaned forward. “Doesn’t she run the register over at the grocery store?”

“That’s her.”

“She seems like a nice girl,” said Murphy. “She always gives me the right change.”

“Isn’t she about three hundred pounds?” asked Walter.

“I’d say she is in that neighborhood,” said Riley.

“Well, then, why are you so interested in losing weight?” asked Walter. “You’re practically twins.”

“I just thought I might stand a better chance with her.”

“I hate to interrupt, but they’re back,” said Murphy. All eyes turned to the McDonald’s restaurant. There was a group of older women sitting at a table near a window. One of the women was staring at the four men sitting on the bench.

“What are we looking at?” asked Riley.

“If you look at that one window, you will see four old women sitting at a table,” said Murphy. “There is one woman in particular staring at us, rather she’s staring at Walter.”

Riley stared intently. “Oh, yes. I see her. Does she have the hots for you, Walter?”

“She used to,” muttered Walter.

“I think she still does,” said Murphy.

“Do we know this lady?” asked Riley.

“She’s Walter’s ex-wife,” said Murphy. “And yes, she still has the hots for Walter.”

“And why wouldn’t she still have a thing for old Walt? Look at what she’s missing out on?” said Walter. “Any woman would be proud as punch to be seen with me.”

“Oh, good Lord,” muttered Sully. “I can’t believe you would even utter such a thing, even in jest.”

"That's just a bit of jealousy on your part," said Walter.

"I don't understand," said Riley. "Why don't you go talk to her? It would seem that there are no hard feelings between you two."

"Why? What's the point?" asked Walter. "I have no intentions of remarrying her. I value my freedom too much."

Walter turned to give her one last look and discovered that she was smiling and waving at him. He half-heartedly waved back until he glanced at Sully and found him waving and smiling as well.

"She's waving and smiling at you, isn't she?" asked Walter.

"I think she wants me," said Sully.

Well, I'll be damned," said Walter. "You steal my little sister's innocence, then I get stuck with you, and now you're about to stick it to my ex-wife. Do you have no shame at all?"

"Did you get any on your first date?" asked Sully still waving.

"I swear to God, Sully," said Walter. "If you don't shut up…"

"You know, I used to drive by and see you guys sitting here and think to myself how much I envied the four of you," said Riley. "I actually believed that you were discussing contemporary issues and sharing historical facts with one another. Little did I know."

"Riley is right," Murphy announced. "Sully, turn around here and leave Gladys alone. Let's discuss something of importance, such as politics or world events."

The four men shifted their bodies on the benches and stared, aimlessly, at the surroundings. Several moments passed by.

"I'm sorry I brought it up," said Riley. "I can't think of a thing."

"Sit tight," said Murphy. "Walter will think of something. In fact, he's always pissin' and moanin' about one thing or another."

All eyes turned to Walter.

"Well, don't look at me," said Walter. "I'm still pissed at numb nuts over here. How I got stuck babysitting your ass for the rest of my life is beyond me. All I know is that God must hate me."

"God doesn't hate you, Walt," said Murphy with a smile. "He just didn't want you to be alone after Gladys left you."

"I'd rather have had a dog," said Walter. "Unlike Sully, a dog wouldn't spew his shit all over the place."

"Okay, so maybe I was wrong," said Riley. "But, hey, from out there in the street, you guys look pretty intellectual."

"Will you stop picking your nose, Walter?" asked Sully.

Murphy jumped to his feet. "On that profound note, I must be going."

"Jesus, Murphy," said Walter. "You want to take a chance and miss some of this?"

"I'll take my chances," said Murphy and walked away.

# Chapter Three

Katherine leaned over and pulled a cake from the oven and set it on the stovetop. The frosting was already prepared in a small bowl, but she wanted the cake to cool before spreading it on.

Murphy opened the backdoor and closed it behind him. He hung up his coat and entered the kitchen. "Boy, something smells good," he said, kissing Katherine on the cheek.

"I'm making you your favorite," she said. "White cake with chocolate frosting."

"What did I do to deserve that?" asked Murphy leaning over the cake.

Katherine's smile disappeared. "It's not what you did. Actually, it's just a little something good to brace you for the bad."

Murphy whipped around and stared at her. "You didn't get the test results back from the doctor, did you?"

"Nothing like that," she said walking across the room. "Come over and sit down."

Even though Murphy was relieved that it apparently had nothing to do with her health, he was puzzled just the same. He pulled out one of the kitchen chairs and sat down.

"Lloyd called this morning," said Katherine with a solemn look.

"Oh," said Murphy with a smile. "How are our grandkids?"

"Lloyd and Helen are getting a divorce," she blurted.

"Oh, my God," muttered Murphy. "What happened?"

"They just can't seem to get along," said Katherine. "They've been married for over twenty years, and according to Lloyd they haven't had even one day without some kind of a fight. Seems as if nobody can get along these days."

"Actually, it isn't a surprise. Seems like that's all they do is fight," said Murphy rubbing his hands together.

"I never thought that Helen was the right one for Lloyd," she said. "She's so loud and overbearing."

Murphy smiled. "That's just like you, Kat," he said. "Rather then call her what she really is, you just gave the dictionary description."

Kat put her hands on her hips. "And what did I just call her?"

"You know very well what you called her."

"No, I don't," she said. "Now, what did I call her?"

"You called her a bitch, Kat," said Murphy nearly laughing aloud.

Katherine smiled. "Why, I would never call another woman such a thing."

"Not in so many words, but the dictionary version works just as well," said Murphy. "By the way, what's going to happen with the kids?"

"Well, that's why Lloyd called," said Katherine. "They want us to take Emmy for the summer."

"Oh, I don't know, Kat," said Murphy. "The last time I saw her, she was quite a handful."

"All young girls go through a change when they become teenagers," said Katherine. "Their bodies and their emotions are in a constant state of change."

"Whoa, hold on there," said Murphy. "That's more information than I needed. Besides, I worry about you. You've got enough going on in your life right now."

A big smile spread across her face as Katherine sat up in her chair. "I'm not going to worry about it anymore. When God's ready to take me home, I've got my bags packed. Until that time, I'm going to enjoy every minute of every day. Besides, I plan to show that doctor that he doesn't know everything."

Murphy slowly shook his head. “I suppose you know that you’ll be the one who will have to put up with her.”

“I wouldn’t have it any other way,” she said. “Besides, I think having her around will take my mind off my own problems.”

Murphy paused as he studied this woman who had been his companion, mate and friend for nearly a half of a century. Life had been good to them, but not without challenges along the way. They had worked hard all their lives and were now ready to enjoy their final years by travelling, resting and enjoying life. Then this came along. This monster called cancer struck without warning. Murphy prayed every night that God would transfer the dreaded disease to his own body and spare this kind and wonderful woman. There were times when it looked as if it had gone into remission, but it would soon rear its ugly head once again. When these times would come and go, it was as if something evil was unmercifully teasing them. They would feel relief and happiness one day, then grief and sorrow the next. The only thing that kept Murphy together was Katherine’s forever smile.

Katherine stared back at him with a look of concern. “Why are you staring at me?”

“Just enjoying the view,” he said with a smile.

“Oh, go on with ya,” she said, turned and walked away.

***

Riley opened the backdoor and eased it shut to avoid waking his mother. He knew that she seldom ever got out of bed and even more seldom was she ever awake.

“Is that you, Riley?” she called out with a crackling voice.

“Yes, Mother,” he replied slowly shaking his head. He knew what was about to follow. She will want to know everything that was said, and, even more importantly, will want to know if they were abusive by ridiculing him about his weight. That would serve as proof that she was right by warning him not to go.

"Come in here for a minute," she said.

Riley sauntered into her bedroom with a disgruntled look on his face. "I know what you're going to ask me and I hate to disappoint you, but I had a great time."

"Why, that's a cruel thing to say," she said, sitting up in bed. "I was just going to ask if you had a good time. That's all."

"Come on, Ma. We both know differently. If they had made fun of me, you would have been proud to say that you told me so."

"Now you're putting words into my mouth, Son," she said. She then coughed raucously and spit into a hankie. "I never said anything like that. I just don't think it looks good for you to be sitting out there on that bench. There is no girl in this town who will have anything to do with you if you spend your time sitting with those old geezers."

"They haven't exactly been breaking my door down as it is," said Riley.

"You're going to meet some nice young girl one of these days," she said. "Just you wait and see."

"Ma, I'm going on sixty-five," he said. "If I do meet some nice young girl, they'll probably throw me in prison."

"Go on. Laugh it up. Make jokes. But I didn't meet your father until I was twenty-three."

"I'm so old I can't remember when I was twenty-three," said Riley. "I know you mean well, but I don't think sitting on a bench for an hour each day is going to spoil my chances to meet Miss Right. Besides, I think I'm going to ask out a certain somebody right here in town."

"Don't tease your mother."

"I'm serious," he said. "I'm going to ask her out just as soon as I work up the nerve."

"And who, may I ask, is this lucky woman?"

"I don't think I should tell you."

"And why not?"

"Because somehow you're gonna screw it up."

"Oh, goodness sakes," she moaned. "There you go again, hurting my feelings. You know I wouldn't do anything…"

"Clara Butts," blurted Riley.

Thelma froze for a moment. "Who?"

"Clara Butts. You know her. She's the cashier over at the grocery store."

"Oh, good Lord, Riley. Why in the world would you want anything to do with her?"

"See. I knew you'd act this way," said Riley. I should have kept it to myself."

"I'm just looking out for your best interests, Son. She's just not for you."

"Ma, I'm not going to sit here and defend her," he said. "I like her enough to want to take her out, and she's been giving me signs that she's interested. That's that. Case closed."

"What could you possibly see in the woman? She's grossly overweight, chews gum while at work, and I sincerely doubt she has ever done a thing with that hair of hers."

"This isn't about you, Mother," he said. "This is about me and my happiness, and if I want your opinion, I'll ask for it."

"I only want the best for you," she said. "By the way, is she a Christian?"

"What?"

"Is she a Christian? Does she go to church?"

"What difference does that make?"

"Who knows? She might be a Jew or an atheist."

"Ma, you haven't been to church since Dad died. That doesn't make you a bad person. Although this conversation is giving me doubts."

"Goodness gracious, Riley, you know I can't go to church. I'm much too sick to even get out of the house."

Riley slowly shook his head. "If I was half as sick as you think you are, I'd probably be dead."

Thelma hurriedly dropped back down on her bed. "I don't have to listen to this. Go ahead and date the tramp if you must. I was only trying to help."

"Ma, it's the same old story," said Riley with a loud voice. "Every time a girl shows an interest in me, and why any girl would is beyond me, you start in on me just like you're doing right now. Either she's too fat or too skinny. She's either too young or too old. You know what I think, Ma? I think you're afraid I'm going to find someone and move out. That's what I think. I think you're afraid you'll lose your little bitch boy, the guy who does everything for you because you're always too sick to get out of bed. Well, you know what? I ain't listening to you no more. From now on, I'm gonna do whatever it takes to find a girl. And maybe, just maybe, if she hangs around longer than one date, I might get laid."

Thelma covered her mouth as she sucked in volumes of air.

"That's right, I'm gonna do my damndest to have sex with a woman," he said. "Sweet Jesus, I'm nearly sixty-five and still a virgin. That just ain't right. It just ain't right. I want to know what it's like to unbutton a woman's shirt and remover whatever they wear under there. I want to know…"

"That's enough, Riley," said Thelma.

"Well, how sad of a case am I? The only naked woman I ever saw was when we were visiting the nursing home and Hazel Crank peeled off her top. Think about that, Ma. The only woman I've seen naked was ninety-eight years old. I only hope the younger ones look better than Hazel."

"Good Lord, Riley," she said. "Give it a rest. You don't discuss such matters with your mother."

"Who should I talk to? Mrs. Crank died three years ago. She was the only woman I was ever intimate with."

"Talk to your dirty-minded friends when you're sitting with them on that bench."

"Oh, yeah," said Riley. "Those guys would love to hear about my affair with Hazel Crank. The only upside of that is I'd have both benches to myself, because the guys would be on the ground laughing their butts off."

Thelma fell back on her bed and sighed. "I swear to God, you're no different than your father. When I think of all the times he whined about not getting any."

"Ma, this is more information than I need," said Riley covering his ears.

"You men are all alike," she said her voice getting louder. "All you ever think about is sex, sex, sex."

Still holding his ears, Riley turned and walked away. "I got to get out of here."

***

It was early afternoon when Walter sat down at the kitchen table. He spread the newspaper on the table and leaned over to read. It wasn't that Walter was that interested in local and world events, more that it was his way of escaping what he considered to be annoying conversation with Sully.

It wasn't so much that he resented Sully for, as he put it, destroying his sister's life, nor was it his offensively effeminate manner; rather it was his constant chatter and self-serving attitude. As Walter observed, Sully was a busybody prying into everybody's business and spending an exorbitant amount of time sharing gossip with just about anyone who would listen.

Walter was understandably upset and to a certain degree distraught when his wife divorced him. It came as no shock to anyone who knew him. He was at the very least crass and offensive. However, his spirits brightened when he experienced for the first time in years quiet and unrelenting solitude. He had forgotten how much he missed being alone. Other than the brief two year marriage, Walter had spent his time by himself and as he described it, "without the annoyance of another resident".

Then, as Sully's marriage turned to divorce, and he lost his home, Walter in a moment of weakness allowed him to spend the night. One thing led to another and soon Sully became that annoying resident.

"Good morning, Walter," said Sully, walking across the kitchen floor.

Walter groaned and turned the page of the newspaper.

"Well, I see we're in a good mood," said Sully.

"What did you expect? It's another day with you."

Sully poured himself a cup of coffee. "Goodness, me, Walter. You know you'll miss me when I move out of here."

"Yeah, like that's ever gonna happen."

"I'm telling you it won't be long now," said Sully. "That friend of mine is placing his mother in a nursing home, and when that happens I'll be out of here for good."

"Okay, Sully. It's time."

"It's time for what?"

"It's time you told me who this friend is," said Walter. "I'd like to know who would let a faggot like you live with him."

"I'm going to disregard that remark and consider from whence it came," said Sully.

"Whence?" said Walter. "Did you say whence? See, that's what I'm talking about. Normal guys don't use that word. Everyday you prove to me that you are one gay bastard."

"Just because I have a command of the English language, that doesn't make me gay."

"Doing the knuckle shuffle on your boyfriend's piss pump does," said Walter.

"That's disgusting."

"No shit," said Walter. "So why do you do it?"

Sully paused with a disgusted look. "So tell me," he said. "What is there about me that makes you think I'm gay?"

"It would be much easier to list the things that make me think you're straight."

"Is it the way I walk or talk?" asked Sully.

"Good Lord, man. You float like a butterfly and say things only a woman would say," said Walter. "I'd bet the house you squat to pee."

"Walter, have you ever seen me with a man?"

"No, but if I ever do, you'll be out on your ass in a heartbeat. I'll be damned if I'm going to have some fudge-packer living with me."

"If I were gay, why would I have married your sister?"

"Well, you got me there," said Walter. "But knowing my sister, I would think she would make a man turn gay."

"You are the most insensitive, vile man I've ever met."

Walter smiled. "I'll bet you say that to all your boyfriends."

"Can we change the subject?" asked Sully with a raised voice.

"That's okay with me," said Walter. "I'm not too thrilled with talking about you and your butt buddies."

"Well then, let me ask you a question, even though I probably know the answer already. What do you think of our new member?"

"He's fat."

"My God," said Sully. "You are so insensitive."

"Don't ask the questions if you don't like the answers."

"I'm talking about his personality, sense of humor, and such."

"He lives with his mother, for Christ's sakes," said Walter. "That pretty much says it all."

Sully smiled. "Well, I think he's kind of handsome."

Walter turned to Sully and slowly shook his head. "How in the world can you say that and deny being a homosexual?"

"Why? What did I say?"

"You know perfectly well what you said. You said that you think he is handsome. Normal guys don't say things like that. Come on, Sully. You're scaring the shit outta me."

Sully began to laugh. "You're just like all the rest," he muttered.

"What are you talking about?"

"A real man can talk about homosexuality around other men," said Sully. "A real man has no doubts or questions about his manhood; therefore, he is free to discuss such issues. Unfortunately, they represent only a small percentage of all men. The rest of you so-called men bluster and become indignant when it comes to the subject of gays. You put up a front to tell the whole world that you are simply appalled by the mere mention of such scum. It's like a defensive measure. It sends a message to all that since you find this obvious contempt for such a lifestyle, you must certainly be straight. You must be an alright guy who loves football, beer and anything with two boobs and a snatch."

"Okay, wise guy," said Walter. "You set up the two categories of men, now which one do you fit into?"

"What do you mean?"

"Are you going to tell me that you are that real man?"

Sully paused. "I'm quite positive that I know what you are going to say, but, yes, I consider myself to be free of inhibitions, proud of my manhood and quite capable of discussing nearly any topic including homosexuality."

"There's a good reason you can talk about homos," said Walter. "Because you are one."

Sully paused. "I thought we were going to talk about Riley."

"Okay, Mister Wise Guy, what do you think of Riley?"

"I told you…"

"And I don't want to hear about how handsome he is," said Walter.

"I think he's intelligent, easy going, but on the downside he seems to have a low self-esteem. I'm sure this can be credited to his lack of independence and a lifestyle that includes living with his mother."

"Since when did you become a head doctor?" asked Walter with a sneer.

"I think it's fairly obvious that the man needs to get out of his mother's house and get his own place."

"Too bad you won't take your own advice," said Walter.

Sully sat down next to Walter. "So, tell me," he said with a sly smile. "Did I hit a nerve when I was waving at Gladys?"

"No. Certainly not," said Walter. "I don't care who you wave at."

"All I know is that you seemed a bit upset when you caught us waving at each other."

"How do you know who she was waving at in the first place?" asked Walter. "She was a long way off and we were close together. She could have been waving at me."

"Why would she? She divorced you. You had your chance, now it's my turn."

"What do you mean your turn?"

"I'm thinking about asking her out."

"You? Why would you ask her out? You don't even like girls."

"I most certainly do like women," said Sully. "I absolutely adore beautiful women."

"Maybe to talk to, but not to have sex with."

"Oh, how soon you forget," said Sully. "I had a child with your sister."

"Trust me," said Walter. "I'll never forget that no matter how hard I try."

"I'll bet you that I could have Gladys in bed within three dates," said Sully.

"Alright. That's enough," said Walter getting to his feet. "I don't want to hear any more talk about sex with Gladys."

"I thought you didn't care."

"I don't."

"I thought you were divorced from her."

"I am."

"So, what's stopping me from taking her out?"

Walter doubled his fist and shook it in Sully's face. "That's what's going to stop you. A knuckle sandwich. Now just drop it before you get hurt."

"So, I guess I did," said Sully with a smile.

"Did what?"

"Struck a nerve."

"You can kiss my hairy ass, you little shit," said Walter as he stormed out the door.

# Chapter Four

It was a little after midnight when it happened. Katherine rolled over in bed and felt a pain in her chest like she had never known. It felt as if someone had his fist wrapped around her heart and was squeezing it with all his might. She paused for several moments hoping it would go away. Instead it seemed to get even more intense. She tried to roll back over but seemed to be frozen in that one spot.

"Murphy," she cried out.

There was no response.

"Murphy," she shouted.

"What?" he muttered.

"I need help."

"What's wrong?"

"I think I'm having a heart attack."

Murphy set up in bed and leaned over her. "What makes you think that?"

"I'm having pains in my chest," she said. "You've got to get me to the hospital."

Murphy froze for just a moment then with a positive voice, he said, "You're as good as there."

The nearest hospital was in Marion, and that was nearly twenty miles away. What normally took thirty minutes to drive to that side of town took Murphy just fifteen. Katherine was carefully transferred onto a gurney and was whisked away to an emergency room. After a brief time of filling out paperwork, Murphy took a seat in the waiting room. He stared at the floor as he tried to collect his thoughts. He'd done his best trying to get Katherine to the hospital in a timely manner. It was a surprise to him that he wasn't pulled over for speeding.

Something was wrong with Katherine, but it didn't make sense. She was suffering from a terminal case of cancer, and yet it would appear that she had just experienced a heart attack. It just didn't add up. Nobody should endure the horror of cancer and have a heart attack as well. It just didn't seem fair.

Murphy ran his hands through his hair and turned to stare out the window. Theirs was not a common marriage. It was unique in many ways. It was holding hands after forty years of marriage. It was notes that said, "I love you" taped to the bathroom mirror and sharing a pizza and a late night movie together. Even after all those years of marriage, they still missed one another when they were separated and felt a certain tinge of excitement when they were reunited.

Most everyone in town knew the Flemmings and jealously wanted a marriage like theirs. When asked the secret of the perfect marriage, Murphy always replied, "There's only one ingredient for a perfect marriage, and that is we never take one another for granted."

It seemed so simple, yet, many never really understood what it meant. Those who did found that it helped their marriage. It didn't matter to Murphy and Katherine. It worked for them, and that's all that mattered.

Murphy began to prepare himself for the worst. The doctor had not given his final diagnosis, but there was always the chance she wouldn't make it. Life seemed so unfair. They had loved each other for so many years, raised a family and had led respectable, Christian lives. Why did God have to take her from him? It almost seemed as if they were being punished for living good lives.

From the other side of the room, a man folded up the newspaper he was reading and held it out in Murphy's direction.

"Wanna see today's paper?" he asked.

"No, thanks," said Murphy.

The man dropped the paper on the chair beside him.

"My name is Archie," said the man.

"Murphy is my name."

"My parents had the nerve to call me Archibald. Can't imagine what they were thinking. At least Archie doesn't sound quite so bad."

Murphy smiled. "At one time, you had your own comic books."

Archie smiled back. "Not many around today would know what you were talking about."

"I suppose you're right," said Murphy. "Those comic books go back as far as the fifties."

There was a pause.

"Got a relative in there?" asked Archie.

"My wife."

"Anything serious?"

"Not sure," said Murphy. "How 'bout you?"

"My dad is in there, believe it or not. He just turned ninety yesterday."

"Is he going to be alright?"

The smile on Archie's face disappeared. "Doesn't look good."

"Sorry to hear that," said Murphy. "At least, you had a lot of good years to spend with your father. Most people don't live that long."

"He's my best friend," said Archie with a sad smile. "He's been my best friend all my life. Ain't that weird? Nobody has his father as his best friend."

"He must be a great guy."

"He is, has been, and always will be the greatest man I ever knew," said Archie.

"What did he do for a living?" Murphy asked.

"He was a college professor."

"That's quite a responsibility," said Murphy. "Did he ever do anything else for a living?"

"Nope. That's all he ever knew," said Archie. "You see, my father loved people, and he especially loved youngsters as they stumbled around trying to learn how to be adults. Thank God for people like my father. Young adults, for the most part, don't get much counseling and leadership from home, and that's where guys like my father come into help."

"If he spent that much time with other young adults, it makes me wonder if he had time for you," said Murphy.

"Oh, that wasn't a problem," said Archie. "He always had time for me. The strange thing about the relationship between my father and me was and is the fact that he treated me like one of his students. I had to sit and be quiet while he talked to me, which was just like being in school."

Murphy smiled. "It's probably a good thing you never had him for a teacher."

"Oh, too late for that," said Archie with a smile. I did go to college, and I did take his class. One would think that the son of the teacher should get an A, but quite the contrary. I failed his class."

"My God! What happened?"

"Dad was always full of surprises, and he sure pulled one on us. You see all though the course, Dad never gave us any tests. He told us that our whole grade relied on the final exam. I'm not sure he was allowed to do that, but Dad wasn't the type who followed the rules. He loved surprising you, but even more important, he loved to genuinely teach you something."

"Obviously, you failed the final exam," said Murphy. "Was it really that hard?"

"Our final exam was one question. Now, mind you, this was an algebra class. One would expect a math question, but not my father. The one question that would determine whether you passed or failed his class was to write down the name of the janitor who worked in that building. We passed by him everyday as we travelled to our classroom, and we were supposed to write down his name. Obviously, we were all upset because we couldn't understand what one thing had to do with the other. I'll never forget my father standing up there and telling us that he could care less if we learned a damn thing about algebra. Math would do very little to prepare us for the real world, but this small lesson would."

Murphy leaned back in his chair. "My God, that's incredible."

"After all these years, I never forgot that lesson, and I seriously think it made a better man of me."

Murphy smiled and slowly shook his head. "That's quite a father you have there."

"I think so," said Archie. "So, now it's your turn. Tell me about your wife."

Murphy blushed. "Oh, I guess the best thing I can say about her is that she has put up with me all these years."

A man dressed in white stepped in the room. "Mr. Flemming?"

"Yes," said Murphy.

"Your wife suffered a very mild stroke. "She wants very much to go home, so we're going to release her, but she needs better care. I gave your wife a card that has the phone number of a place that can provide you with someone to stay at your house and take care of her."

"Can I see her now?" Murphy asked as he shook Archie's hand.

"Room one twelve."

Murphy walked down the hallway and turned into one of the rooms. Except for a lamp near the bed, it was completely dark. Katherine was sitting up in her bed.

"Hi, Kat," said Murphy. "How are you doing?"

"I'm fine," she said. "Now get me out of here."

"Are you sure you should…"

"Yes, I'm sure. I've already got my clothes on. Let's get out of here. I belong at home."

Murphy stared at her for a moment then grabbed the wheelchair. "Let's go home."

***

It was late morning when Riley Hoagland parked his car in front of Lingos Dry Goods Store. He got out of his car and walked over to the two men sitting on the two benches.

"Good morning, Gentlemen," said Riley.

"Friggin' Murphy is late again," said Walter with a frown.

"I guess we can skip the formalities," muttered Riley.

Sully pointed at his own bench and said, "Sit next to me. Walt is being a real shit today."

"Even worse than normal?" asked Riley.

"I hope both of you shit the bed tonight and roll in it," said Walter.

"I guess that answers my question," said Riley.

"Don't sit too close to Sully," said Walter. "You might catch some kind of homo disease like herpes or whatnot."

"What's got you in a tizzy, Walt?" asked Riley.

"Murphy is always here on time, and he ain't here at all."

"Maybe he's sick or something," said Riley.

"Murphy never gets sick," said Walter. "So where the hell is he?"

"Car problems?"

"Ahhhh. Something ain't right, I'm telling ya. I've known Murphy all my life, and I know there's a problem."

Riley turned to Sully. "Should we be concerned?"

"Walter over there has enough concern for all of us," said Sully.

"I don't know, but I always thought that sitting out here on this geezer bench was supposed to be fun," said Riley. "Seems as if all we do is bitch about stuff."

Walter turned to Riley with a puzzled look. "What did you call this bench?"

"The geezer bench."

Walter said nothing. He continued to stare at Riley as if he had horns.

"Hey, I didn't make it up," said Riley. "Everyone in town calls this the geezer bench and the guys sitting on it geezers."

"I don't mind being called a geezer," said Sully.

"I can believe that," said Walter. "Better than being called a faggot."

"You'll be surprised to know that people don't call me that," said Sully. "You're the only one who is so insensitive to refer to me in such a vile manner."

"I'm the only one who calls you that to your face," said Walter. "The others call you a queer behind your back."

Riley slapped his knees with both hands. "Wow! This sure is going good this morning."

"I don't know what you were expecting," said Sully. "But this is about as good as it gets. "As long as we have cranky old geezers like Walter here, we're going to have a lot of bitching."

Walter pointed at a car across the street. An overweight woman was struggling to get out of it. "Isn't that Clara Butts getting out of that car?"

The other two stared at the woman but said nothing.

"Isn't she the one you have the hots for, Riley, my boy?" Walter asked.

"I didn't say that I had the hots for…"

"Want me to call her over here?"

"No, Walter. Just let it drop.

"Hey, I don't mind at all," said Walter as he turned back to Clara. "Hey, Clara. Come over here for a minute."

She studied the three men for a moment then began to waddle across the street.

"Jesus, Walter," said Riley with a sheepish grin. "I can't believe you did that."

Clara was panting by the time she reached the benches. “What do you want, Walter? I need to get to work.”

“Well, I think I have good news for you,” said Walter with a smile.

Riley squirmed on his seat and soon turned in another direction.

“Come on, Walter,” she said. “Out with it.”

“Riley over here wants to take you out on a date,” said Walter pointing at Riley.

Clara turned to Riley. “Why isn’t he telling me this?”

Riley turned back around. “Don’t pay any attention to Walter. He’s been sniffing his socks again.”

“Do you mean it ain’t true?” she asked.

“I didn’t say that.”

“What did you say?”

“I’m just saying that Walter had no business butting in like that,” said Riley.

“Well, do you want to take me out or not?”

“Good Lord, Clara,” said Riley. “I’m over sixty, and you can’t be more than…”

“What’s that mean?” she asked. “Are you trying to tell me you might need help crossing the street?”

“No, I was just trying to…”

“Here, let me make it easy on ya,” she said. “Pick me up around six next Friday night. You’re taking me out to the diner then whatever else we decide on.”

Riley froze. He said nothing.

“Well? Are we good?”

“Yeah. Sure. I’ll be there,” said Riley still wearing a stunned look.

“I gotta get to work,” said Clara walking away from the men. “Go on back to doing whatever it is you old turds do.”

Riley smiled as he watched her walk away.

"You owe me, buddy," said Walter. "If it wasn't for me, you would be destined to play with yourself for the rest of your life."

Riley turned with a frown. "I'm taking her to dinner. I'm not having sex with her."

"Good Lord, man," said Walter. "That's the way it gets started. You throw a few bucks at her, blow smoke up her skirt and the next thing you know she's riding the baloney pony."

"Oh, for God's sakes, Walter," said Riley. "We're just going out for a bite to eat. People don't have sex on the first date."

"Where the hell have you been?" Walter asked. "Hell, the women today expect to get laid. Most of them are hornier than we are. The days of the Leave It To Beaver mom in her perfectly ironed dress and pearls around her neck are sadly gone."

"Aren't we exaggerating a bit?"

"Good Lord, look around you," said Walter. "Today's woman wears men's clothes, even baseball caps. They drive big trucks and cuss so much I can't believe they eat with their mouths. Femininity died a long time ago."

Sully laughed. "You don't know the first thing about females. You treated Gladys like she was the hired help."

"You got me there," said Walter. "You would know everything there is to know about females 'cause you are one."

"Hey, guys," said Riley. "Can we stop this shit for just a minute, so I can enjoy the fact that I am going on my first date?"

"Your first date!" said Walter, trying to hold back the laughter. "This is your first date?"

"Don't start with me, Walter. I'm really enjoying the moment, now don't wreck it."

"I don't friggin' believe it. Nobody has ever lived over sixty years and not gone out on a date," said Walter. "Hell, even the queer bait here was even married to a woman, for God's sakes."

"My God! You are such an animal," said Sully. He turned to Riley. "Don't pay any attention to Mister Sensitivity over here. Miss Butts seems to be a nice young lady, so just enjoy your date with her."

"Oh, my God!" said Riley. "I need to prepare for my date. What should I do to get ready?"

Sully turned and studied him for a moment. "You might want to get a haircut, if nothing else."

"You might want to drop about two hundred pounds in the next week," said Walter.

Sully gave Walter a dirty look and turned back to Riley. "Be certain that your fingernails are trimmed and clean. Women notice such things."

"If Sully noticed your fingernails, that means any other female would too," said Walter.

"Anything else?" asked Riley.

Sully paused for a moment. "I wouldn't worry too much about it. Just be yourself and everything will turn out just fine. From what little I know about Miss Butts, I just can't imagine she is all that meticulous about presentation.

"What does that mean?" asked Riley.

"It means she's a pig," said Walter.

Riley got to his feet. "I think I'll go home and do some exercises. Maybe I can lose a pound or two by next week."

"Good luck with that," mumbled Walter.

"Sully, it's been nice talking with you," said Riley. "Walter…you are one in a million. Thank God!"

Walter said nothing as he watched Riley waddle towards his truck.

"Do you think he meant that as a compliment?" asked Walter.

"What are you talking about?" asked Sully.

"That business about the one in a million. Do you think he meant that as a compliment?"

Sully slowly shook his head. "Come on, Walt. Let's go home."

## Chapter Five

Murphy turned into his driveway and stopped the car at the front door. He winced and shook his head when he saw his son and granddaughter already sitting on the front porch with two oversized pieces of luggage beside them. Murphy quickly got out of the car and ran around to open the passenger-side door.

"Murphy, will you quit fussing over me?" Katherine asked.

He placed his arm around her shoulders and helped her to the porch.

"Hi, folks," said Lloyd.

Murphy nodded his head. "Come over here and get the door."

Lloyd ran over and opened the door while Murphy helped her cross the threshold. He then led her across the room and eased her into a soft leather chair.

"It's so good to be back home," she said with a sigh.

"Is there anything I can get you?" Murphy asked.

"No," she said with a stern voice. "Sit down and stop fretting over me."

Murphy pulled a straight-back chair over near Katherine and sat down.

Lloyd stared at the two of them with a puzzled look. "Are you okay, Mother?"

"Hell, no, she's not okay," barked Murphy.

"Watch your language, Murphy," she said. "There are young ears in here with us."

"Well, what's wrong, Mom?" Lloyd asked. "Did something happen with your cancer?"

"As if your mother doesn't have enough problems, she had a heart attack," said Murphy.

"Oh, my God!" said Lloyd. "You had a heart attack, Mother?"

Katherine waved her hand. "It wasn't anything serious. I'll be fine."

"All heart attacks are serious, Kat," said Murphy.

"Jeez. Now I kinda feel bad about asking you to watch Emmy for the summer," muttered Lloyd.

Murphy turned and leaned towards his son. "Lloyd, under the circumstances, I don't think it would be such a great idea to…"

"Never you mind, the two of you," said Kat. "She'll be fine. We'll all be fine. I think it will do me good to have a young one around the house again."

Murphy turned to Emmy. "What about it, Emmy? What do you think about all of this?"

The young teenage girl got to her feet and folded her arms. "I do whatever my wonderful father tells me to do," she said with a disgusted look on her face and stormed out the front door.

"What was that all about?" asked Murphy.

"She's a bit upset with her mother and me over this whole thing," said Lloyd.

"Well, I don't want her acting like that around us."

"She's a teenage girl," said Katherine. "All teenage girls go through a period where they are a bit unruly and hard to understand."

"She acts like she needs her butt swatted," said Murphy.

"Things have changed, Dad," said Lloyd. "It isn't the same as it was back years ago. If I was to spank her and she told her teacher, I'd be in jail in no time."

"That doesn't surprise me," said Murphy. "It's a crazy world anymore."

"If you don't mind my asking, what happened between you and Helen?" asked Katherine.

"I don't know," he said. "We just sort of went in different directions. She had her career and I had mine. Then when the kids came along, that just seemed to separate us even more. The next thing I knew, I was living with a stranger."

"For God's sakes, Lloyd, try patching it up with your wife," said Murphy. "What you just described can be fixed with a little work. You know that you have to work at a marriage for it to succeed, don't you?"

"I have a girlfriend, Pop," said Lloyd.

Murphy froze as he stared at him for several moments. "What did you say?"

"I have a girlfriend, and I hope to marry her someday."

"Son, I don't know how to break this to you, but they frown on having two wives in this country."

"I plan to divorce Helen first."

Murphy turned to Katherine. "Do you believe what you're hearing? Things get a little bumpy, and we bail out. Thank God, we never had rough spots along the way."

"I knew you'd be upset with me, Pop. I didn't want to tell you, but I guess you should know."

"Does Helen know about your sleazy friend?" Murphy asked.

"Actually, that's the reason we're getting a divorce," said Lloyd. "She caught us together."

"Good God!" said Murphy. "This story only gets worse as we go along."

"Murphy!" shouted Katherine. "Come over here." She motioned for him to lean over so that she could whisper in his ear. "Let it go, Murphy. He's got enough problems without you dragging him through the mud as well. Emmy is staying here for the summer, and that's that."

Murphy slowly pulled away. He started to say something, but she pointed a finger at him as if to tell him to mind her.

"Okay, Son," said Murphy. "Emmy can stay with us for the summer. Can't say that I won't kill her before it's all over."

"Thanks, folks. I really appreciate this. I'll say goodbye to her and be on my way."

Lloyd stepped out onto the porch to find Emmy sitting on the porch swing. Her arms were still folded, and she was staring at the ground. Murphy watched as his son approached her.

"I have to go now, Emmy," he said leaning over to her. "Grandpa and Grandma have agreed to take care of you for the summer. I'll be around from time to time to see how you're doing."

"Why bother?" she blurted.

"Now, you behave while you're here," said Lloyd. "Grandpa and Grandma don't need any more headaches right now."

Lloyd stared at here expecting some acknowledgement. She didn't flinch. He walked over to Murphy and shook his hand. "Thanks again, Pop," he said and walked away.

As soon as he had driven away, Emmy stood and walked over to Murphy. "I hope you don't think you can bully me around just because you're old," she said, then stormed off the porch and down the road.

***

Thelma Hoagland had been married nearly all her life or so it seemed to Mr. Hoagland. They had been married nearly fifty years when Mr. Hoagland passed away. It was a kind and gentle death. He simply went to bed one night and didn't wake up the next morning. Many of his close friends said that he had been praying for years for such an event, and why wouldn't he? Everyone in town knew what Thelma was like. She was always sick with some sort of malady and made damn sure you knew all about it, including the sometimes sordid details. No one had ever seen her laugh, or for that matter, had even seen a grin on her face. She usually carried a look of distress on her face that was meant to tell the world that she was sick with some form of illness, if not some little-known disease. Fortunately for the local citizens, she was bedridden and was seldom seen outside of the house. With her son living with her, she always had someone to fetch whatever she needed or desired. Actually, Riley didn't mind being her personal slave, seeing as how he had taken care of her all of his life. He simply didn't know any other life.

Thelma swung her feet out of the bed and placed them gently on the floor. She grabbed a cane that was leaning against the wall and started walking towards the bathroom. As she stepped out of her bedroom and into the living room, she was confronted with Riley sitting upright in the middle of the floor.

"What in God's name are you doing?" she asked.

"Sit ups," he barked. "I'm doing sit ups."

"What the hell for?"

"Why do you think I'm doing them? I'm trying to lose weight."

Riley leaned back and struggled to lift himself forward.

"You're going to kill yourself in the process."

Almost completely out of breath, he managed to return to an upright position and leaned back with his hands on the floor. "Well, then, so be it."

Thelma stared at him as he struggled to do another one. "Goodness sakes, boy, what's got into you? Why the sudden interest in killing yourself?"

"I got a date," he said with a smile."

"What?"

"I got a date in a few days, and I want to lose a few pounds."

"Who in the world would go out with you?"

"Thanks, Ma. I needed that."

"You're not going out with some farm animal, are you?"

"For God's sakes, Mother! That's disgusting! I'm taking Clara Butts out."

"Oh, good Lord, Son. That's the same as taking out a farm animal. In fact, a farm animal would have more manners. Can't you do any better than Clara Butts?"

"Mother, women are not exactly breaking down my door. I'm over sixty years old and this is my first date. I'll take what I can get."

"She's trash, Riley. Simply trash."

"I don't care, Mother. Hell, if she is trash, there's a good chance I might get laid, and I would do just about anything to make that happen."

"Men are such pigs," she said and hobbled off to the bathroom.

Riley leaned back and grunted out another sit up. "Well, this is one pig that's gonna get his sow."

After a few minutes in the bathroom, she started across the floor in front of Riley. "Oh, I don't feel so good, my son," she said holding her head with one hand and the cane with the other.

Riley slowly got to his feet and leaned over to catch his breath. "Damn, my stomach feels tighter."

"I said I don't feel so good," said Thelma with a bit louder voice.

"I heard ya," said Riley feeling his stomach.

"Well, aren't you going to do something?"

"Yeah, I'm going to try and do some push ups."

Thelma waved at him and turned towards her bed. "I swear to God if I had it to do over, I'd have aborted that child."

***

Sully walked into the living room where Walter was watching television. The sound was turned up, and Walter was nearly asleep. Sully sat down in a rocking chair next to Walter.

"Guess who called and asked me out," said Sully.

Walter batted his eyes several times and sat up in his chair. "Don't know and don't care," he said.

"It was Gladys," said Sully with a grin.

"Bullshit!"

"I'm telling you the truth. She called me and asked me to go out with her."

"Number one, she is doing this just to make me jealous, and number two, you're a gay little prick and would only go out with her to get back at me."

"That's not true," said Sully. "I like Gladys and think we might have much in common. There's a good possibility we could develop a very meaningful relationship."

"The only meaningful relationship you could have with any woman would be swapping recipes."

"I think you're in for a big surprise, Mr. Smarty Pants," said Sully. "I think she wants to have sex with me."

"Gladys could care less about sex."

"That's probably because you don't know how to take care of a woman," said Sully. "There's an art to doing it correctly so that she is satisfied as well."

"What makes you think I don't know how to take care of a woman?" Walter asked with a defensive tone.

"Because I know you," said Sully. "You're only a notch above a primal ape."

"So, what you're telling me is that you know how to please a woman. Is that right?"

"Absolutely."

"You do remember that women are the ones without the penis."

Sully slowly shook his head. "Why is it you always return to my being gay? Is there some reason for that?"

"The only reason I can think of is because it's true," said Walter.

"You tease Riley because he's overweight and you continually accuse me of being gay. Why do you find so much pleasure in ridiculing others?"

"I'm merely pointing out the truth," said Walter.

"But your opinion of the truth is never requested," said Sully. "I don't share my opinion of you with everyone. I have more consciousness and sensitivity than that."

The smile disappeared from Walter's face. "And what is your opinion of me?"

"Well, since you asked, I don't mind telling you. You are a self-centered, egotistical brute with absolutely no social graces at all. Your insensitive approach to people alienates you to all but the very few who can tolerate such behavior. The only thing I can say in your behalf is that all of these unacceptable and hideous traits of yours can be explained by your incredible lack of brain power which must put you somewhere close to a moronic state. Actually, I'm quite positive that if a few tests were administered, we'd discover that you very certainly are retarded."

Walter paused as he stared at Sully. "I'm not real sure what you said, but I did hear the word moron in there somewhere."

"Let me put it in terms you'll understand," said Sully. "You must stop teasing people. It not only annoys them, it alienates you from the crowd."

"Huh?"

"It pisses off people, and they consequently don't like you," said Sully in frustration.

"Yeah, but I'm just having fun," said Walter.

"You don't get it, do you?" said Sully. "The problem is you're having fun at someone else's expense. You belittle others to make you feel better about yourself.

Deep down, you know you are a social misfit, you have accomplished very little in your pathetic life and will more than likely go to the grave with only a handful of mourners at your gravesite. So to compensate for your failure as a human being, you try to bring others down to your disgraceful level of existence. Simply put for your small brain to understand, you are getting an ego boost at the expense of others. In a word, you are pathetic."

Walter gritted his teeth and shook a fist in Sully's face. "I'd ought to kick your little faggot ass."

"Oh, let's see. You take offense at someone pointing out your faults and misgivings. Who does that sound like?"

"Yeah, but what I say is funny," said Walter lowering his fist.

"Only to you," said Sully. "Nobody else thinks so."

"Well, then, why is everyone laughing at what I say?"

"It's a nervous, defensive laughter," said Sully. "They don't want to be your next target, so they jump on your band wagon to avoid becoming your next victim. To put it bluntly, you're a bully. It's as simple as that."

Walter smiled. "So, you think I'm a bully."

"Oh, God! I just stroked your ego, didn't I?"

"Call it what you like," said Walter as he turned and walked away. "But I'm good with being a bully."

## Chapter Six

The next morning found Murphy already sitting on the bench when Walter and Sully got out of their truck. They slowly walked over to him and took a seat across from him.

"Well, look who's back," said Walter.

"Morning," said Murphy. "How are we doing?"

"Better yet," said Sully. "How are you doing? It's rather uncommon for you to miss a day on the geezer bench."

Just then, an older truck pulled up, and a large, overweight man struggled to get out of the cab.

"Let's wait until Riley gets seated, so that I don't have to say this twice," said Murphy.

Walter smiled as he watched Riley climb out of his truck. "My God, what a load," he muttered softly. "Did you see that truck bounce back up when he got out? It's probably sighing from relief."

"Morning, guys," said Riley standing straight and with his hands on his hips. "Notice anything different?"

"The three men paused as they studied him.

"New shoes?" asked Sully. "A man can never have too many shoes."

"That's what women say, dumbass," said Walter. "Men have a brown pair and a black pair and that's all. More proof that you're gay."

"I can see our little talk yesterday did some good," said Sully.

"Lose some weight?" asked Murphy.

"Three pounds," said Riley beaming with pride.

"I've taken dumps that weighed more than that," muttered Walter.

"On a diet?" asked Murphy.

"Oh, you don't know because you weren't here yesterday," said Riley taking a seat on one of the benches. "I have a date with Clara Butts."

"If it hadn't been for me, it would never had happened," said Walter.

"For once, you're right," said Sully. "In your own crude, barbaric way, you were instrumental in getting them together."

"So, you have a date with Clara Butts," said Murphy with a smile. "That's fantastic."

Riley lightly struck his stomach with his fist. "I've been doing sit ups, too. Man, do my stomach muscles hurt."

"They probably hurt from being stretched so far," muttered Walter.

"Where are you taking her?" asked Murphy.

"Well, I was thinking about taking her to the diner then over to Marion to watch a movie."

"Oh, good Lord," said Walter. "You're going to have to do better than that if you want to get laid."

Riley said nothing. He turned to Murphy for advice.

"Dinner and a movie would be just perfect," said Murphy. "That's what Clara would expect and would like. Anything fancier wouldn't appeal to her."

"Are you sure?" asked Riley.

"I'm sure."

"By the way, is everything okay at home?" asked Riley. "We were worried about you since you didn't show yesterday."

"We had a little scare yesterday," said Murphy. "Kat had a minor heart problem, and just to be safe I took her into the hospital."

"Is she okay?" asked Sully.

"She's fine. The only problem is they are sending over a nurse to stay with us. They said she needs twenty-four hour care."

"That sounds like a good idea, Murphy," said Riley. "Why are you calling it a problem?"

"I just can't stand the idea of someone living with us. It's like having an intruder staying with us."

"I'd think you would be thrilled to have a nurse nearby," said Riley.

Murphy slowly shook his head as if trying to understand his own feelings. "I just want these last few days to be good for Kat. I don't need an audience watching what should be a very private time between Kat and me. We've been together nearly all our lives, and when her time comes, I want to be there with her. I want my heart next to hers when it stops beating. That's not too much to ask. A man should be there when his life-long mate leaves this earth. I should be there, holding her and giving her as much comfort as I can."

The other three grew silent. They gave each other quick, solemn looks but mainly lowered their heads in silence.

"I didn't mean to put a damper on things," said Murphy. "It's just that for the first time in my life, I don't want to think about the future. For now, I will treasure every day that God grants Kat and me."

Out of respect, none of the others spoke. It was Murphy's time, and no one wanted to take it away from him.

"To make matters worse, my granddaughter is spending the summer with us," said Murphy.

The others fidgeted in their seats trying to find the right thing to say.

"Sorry, Murphy," said Riley. "That can't be good."

"No, it's not good. She doesn't want to be there, and she has a real snotty attitude."

"Why is she there?" asked Riley.

"Her parents are getting a divorce, and they don't want to deal with her. I personally think they're using the divorce as an excuse to get rid of her for a while. Ever since she became a teenager, she's had an incredibly bad attitude about everything."

"Most all teenage girls go through a stage like that," said Sully. "I heard it once said that better they go through it while they are young rather than ruining a man's life after they are grown."

To the surprise of all, Walter didn't comment on Sully's statement. He remained silent.

Murphy slapped his hands together and sat up straight. "Let's talk about something else. Walter, are you ever going to take Agnes out again?"

"I don't think so," said Walter. "Agnes flat out told me she hasn't had sex in over forty years. There's a real good chance that thing has healed shut from lack of use. I don't see a future with her."

"See that's the problem with you, Walter," said Sully. "You don't know what's important in life. Agnes might very well be the perfect companion, one who could make you smile and take care of you as you grow older."

"There's only one thing I want her to take care of, and I got a feeling that ain't gonna happen."

"So, your only reason for getting married is to have someone there to take care of you when you have the need?" asked Sully.

"Why else would a man get married?" Walter replied.

"For love, companionship and friendship."

"If that's all I needed, I'd get a dog," said Walter. "I just want someone to nail once in a while."

"My God, you are such a pig," said Sully.

"I got to take Sully's side on this one," said Riley. "I can't imagine a marriage lasting very long if it was based solely on sex."

"How would you know?" said Walter. "You're still a virgin."

"Gentlemen, gentlemen," said Murphy. "Let's think of something else to talk about."

There was a pause as each man traded glances.

"We could always talk about religion," blurted Walter.

"Oh, no," said Murphy. "We agreed a long time ago not to talk about politics or religion."

"That's not such a good idea," said Riley.

"Why not?" asked Walter.

"It usually leads to arguments and hard feelings."

"Well, I'd rather talk about religion than your going on your first date."

"Okay, you want to talk about religion, you start it off," said Riley.

"Hell, that's easy," said Walter. "There is no God. Case closed."

"I should have known," muttered Riley.

"I know I'm going to regret this, but on what evidence or premise do you base your belief?" asked Sully.

"The same evidence you believers have…none."

"Well, you must have some criteria for basing your decision."

"What the hell are criteria?"

"You must have some reasons for not believing in God," said Sully.

"Okay, Mr. Smarty Pants, you tell me all about the evidence you have for believing in God."

Riley turned and held up a hand to Sully. "Because you are so ignorant of religion and haven't taken the time to learn about it, it's actually quite useless to discuss it with you. You want evidence? There is no tangible evidence for you to hold in your hands. That's probably the most important thing you need to learn. God made it really simple. He gave us ten rules to follow and told us to have faith in him. That's it. Nothing complicated to it. Ten rules and believe in Him."

"Well, I don't get it," said Walter.

Murphy turned and leaned forward. "That's the whole point of why He told us to have faith in Him. You don't get it…we all don't get it. Nobody understands because of the limited brain power that we humans have. We think we have the ultimate thinking machine. Largely because we compare our brains with the brains belonging to farm animals. God limited our brain power to a level that will sustain us here on earth. We know enough to zip up when we're done and to hold back a fart in public. In the whole scheme of things, we are a very primitive species."

"Good Lord, Murphy," said Walter. "We sure hit a nerve on you. You should have been a preacher."

"Like I said before, we need to keep religion and politics out of the picture," said Murphy.

"I didn't even know you were the religious sort," said Walter. "When did you get so holier-than-thou?"

"I think it was when I read something that Albert Einstein wrote. He said that you'd have to be a fool not to believe that thought went into all of this. Whether you believe in God or not, that statement is true."

Walter waved his hand at Murphy. "Einstein, God and whatnot. This stuff is way over my head. Let's find something else to talk about."

Riley turned to Walter with a smile. "Right after you went on your first date with Agnes, you declared that you were going to date her again. Now it would seem that you've changed your mind. What happened?"

"I just told you that I don't think she'd be any good in bed."

"How do you know unless you give her a try?" Riley asked.

"Besides, I don't see that many women busting down your door," said Sully.

"Good Lord," said Walter. "Why is everyone so interested in my love life?"

"Because your love life is non-existent," said Sully. "And knowing you as well as we do, we understand why. It's hard to believe that any woman would have any interest in you, especially Agnes Dutton."

"Maybe, you're right," said Walter. "Maybe if I throw a meal and a movie at her, she might put out."

Sully stared at Walter. "Another sensitive statement by an incredibly sensitive man."

Murphy got to his feet. "I gotta go, gentlemen. I'll miss this stimulating conversation, but I have things to do."

"Take care, Murph," said Riley.

"Have a great day," said Murphy as he got in his truck and drove away.

It was a long drive home for Murphy. For the first time, he was not at all anxious to get there. With his granddaughter living there and the possibility of a nurse moving in, he felt somewhat violated by this unwanted intrusion. It had been years since their boys had left home, and both Murphy and Kat had grown accustomed to having their home all to themselves. Murphy knew that under normal circumstances, it would only be a short period of time to make an adjustment, but with Kat's current medical condition, he didn't have the time. It was also a great concern of Murphy that Kat and he have these last few days to themselves. After all, they had been together for nearly all their lives, and time was running out. There was much to be said, feelings to be shared and they certainly didn't want an audience.

"Morning, everybody," said Murphy walking through the front door.

Emmy was watching television in the living room. She did nothing to even acknowledge his arrival.

"Where's your grandmother?" he asked.

Emmy simply thrust a pointed thumb over her shoulder.

Murphy headed straight for the bedroom to find Kat lying in bed.

"Are you okay?" he asked.

"I feel fine," she replied.

"Why are you in bed?"

"Our resident nurse is here, and she insisted that I get in bed."

"Well, why would you go to bed if you feel fine?"

"She didn't say."

"Well, why did you do it?"

"You'll understand when you meet Belva Burke."

It was about that time that a black woman dressed in a white nurse's uniform stepped into the room. She was middle-aged, very short, and extremely overweight. She wore a sneer and half closed eyes that had years ago become her trademark.

Murphy extended his hand. "You must be Miss Burke."

She gave him a quick glance then nudged by him to set a glass of water and two pills on the table beside the bed. "Must be," she mumbled.

Murphy slowly returned his hand to his side. "Miss Burke, can you tell me why you have confined Kat to a bed?"

"I ain't confined nobody to a bed. She can get up if she wants."

"Okay, let me rephrase this," said Murphy. "Why did you suggest that she go to bed?"

"In case you haven't noticed, your wife is very sick and needs lots of rest," she said picking up clothes from the floor. "Mrs. Flemming, I'm gonna do a load of wash and will be right back. Mr. Flemming, if you're wonderin' where your lunch is, it's somewhere out there in the kitchen. You'll find it in the fridge or the pantry. Just depends on what you know how to fix."

"Well, ain't she a peach?" he said as he watched her walk out of the room.

"I like her," said Kat.

"You do?" blurted Murphy. "Then, you must love hemorrhoids."

"She might be a little rough around the edges, but I'll bet she's a good nurse."

"Kat, sometimes you can be so naïve," he said with a grin. I'll bet you think Adolph Hitler was a great guy."

Kat pulled back the blanket and started to get out of bed.

"Where are you going?" Murphy asked.

"I'm going to fix you something to eat."

"Oh, no, you don't," said Murphy pulling the blanket back over her. "Our own resident Hitler would probably kick me out of the house. I'll fix something. By the way, can I fix you something as well?"

"No, Belva has already made me breakfast."

Murphy paused. "You mean to tell me she fixed you something, but she won't do the same for me?"

Kat smiled. "Isn't she the greatest?"

Belva stepped into the kitchen and stopped in the middle of the room. She scanned the counter tops and the sink. She continued into the living room only to find Emmy eating breakfast as she watched television.

"Were you just in the kitchen?" Belva asked with a gruff voice.

Emmy turned to her two pieces of toast and then back to Belva. "What do you think?"

"Get your ass up and go clean up your mess," she barked.

"What?"

"You heard me," said Belva. "You're not gonna move in here and treat your grandparents that way."

"Who do you think you are?" Emmy asked.

"I think I'm the one who will beat your ass if you don't clean up that kitchen," she said.

"You can't talk to me that way."

Belva marched across the room and stopped in front of her. She picked the two pieces of toast from her plate, walked over to the front door and threw them into the yard. "Now, I'm done talking," she said and started for Emmy with doubled fists. Emmy jumped to her feet and ran into the kitchen.

Minutes later, Murphy stepped into the kitchen to fix himself something only to find Emmy washing crumbs from the countertop. "Well, how nice of you to…"

"Who the hell does that woman in a nurse's uniform think she is?" Emmy blurted.

"Why? What happened?"

"She threatened to beat my ass."

"Why did she do that?"

"She told me I had to come in here and clean the kitchen."

"Didn't you make the mess?"

"Well, isn't it her job to clean it up?"

Murphy pulled out a chair and sat down at the table. "Sit down, Emmy," he said.

She stared at Murphy for a moment, then threw the dishcloth in the sink and sat down. Immediately, she folded her arms and looked past her grandfather with a sneer on her face.

"Now I know you don't want to be here," said Murphy. "And quite frankly this couldn't have happened at a worse time. Your grandmother is dying, and I just don't need any outside aggravations right now. All I ask is that you behave yourself and try to be a little understanding. The only good thing about this attitude thing you've got going on is that you're quiet, and I need plenty of that right now. As far as Miss Burke is concerned, she's here to take care of your grandmother. She isn't your personal maid.

The only reason she helps out is because that's common courtesy. She's considerate enough to realize that if you are staying in somebody's house, you need to pull your own weight, which is something I would hope you would come to realize."

There was a long and silent pause. Murphy stared at her, waiting for a reaction. Finally, she turned slightly in his direction.

"Are you finished?" she snapped.

"I think so," said Murphy.

"May I go now?"

"You can go right after you tell me why you are giving me this attitude," said Murphy. I'm not the one who kicked you out. I'm the one who took you in. Can you at least tell me what I did to deserve this?"

Emmy turned towards her grandfather. "Because I don't want to be here. Just because my father has to have a girlfriend, I have to leave my house and all my friends. It just isn't fair."

"Well, I can't say as I blame you, Emmy, but your fight is with your dad, not us," said Murphy.

"May I go now?" she asked, starting to get to her feet.

Murphy sighed. "Yes, you may go now." He frowned as he watched her walk away.

***

On the other side of town, Walter was sitting at his kitchen table. He was drinking coffee and reading the paper when Sully walked in carrying a grocery bag with something inside.

"What 'cha got there?" Walter asked.

Sully opened the bag and poured out an array of lottery tickets onto the table.

"What the hell you got there?" Walter asked.

"Lottery tickets," Sully announced.

"Lottery tickets," said Walter. "Since when did you become a gambler?"

"Since realizing that I'm never going to get out of here if I don't acquire a sizeable amount of money," said Sully with a look of pride. "Buying these was so demeaning. I felt like white trash."

"Why did that make you feel like white trash?"

"I always thought that only losers bought these ghastly things," said Sully. "I'm surprised you don't buy them on a regular basis."

Walter paused. "Did you just call me a loser?"

"How perceptive of someone with an I.Q. as low as yours."

"Did you just call me dumb?"

"There's that perception thing again," said Sully with a smile.

Walter turned back to the tickets strewn across the table. "Well, I'll have to admit that for once in your life you've got a good idea."

"As soon as I hit the big one, I can afford to move out of here," said Sully. "You'll be happy, and I can guarantee you I will be thrilled to death."

"Sounds like a plan," said Walter sipping his coffee. "What kinds do you have?'

"I have all different kinds," said Sully. "I have the rub-off kind for winning instantly and then the kind where they announce the winning numbers."

Walter turned to stare blankly at the ceiling with a smile. "I can see it all now. I see a day in the near future when I'll have the whole house to myself. There'll be no straight guys, no queers, just me and the four walls."

Sully picked up a coin and began scraping the coating from the tickets. When he had finished, he held the ticket and studied it for a moment. "Well, we weren't quite so lucky on our first one."

Walter grabbed it from his hand and glanced at it. "Why the hell are you even bothering with this? The most you can make is fifty bucks."

Sully turned with a smile. "These are to net us some extra money so that we can purchase the other kind of ticket."

"By God, you've thought of everything," said Walter. "Just don't get my hopes up and then somehow fail to win some money."

"I don't know how we could lose," said Sully pointing at the scattered tickets on the table. "We have this kind of ticket that will make us rich, and these over here will generate the money to buy them. How could we go wrong?"

With a big smile which was rare for Walter, he lightly patted Sully on the back. "It won't be long now. You might as well start packing."

***

Riley leaned over and groaned as he tried to touch the floor with his hands. He straightened himself and then tried again, this time coming even closer.

"What are you doing in there?" shouted Thelma from her bedroom.

"I'm exercising," he replied with a voice that was gasping for air.

"Don't tell me you're still planning on taking that tramp out on a date?"

"That's the plan, Mother."

"Stop that silliness and come in here," she snapped.

Riley stood straight and with a frown slowly walked into her bedroom. "I'm kinda busy here. What do you want?"

"I've done some checking on that slut that you plan to take out on a date," she said with an air of indignation. "You know she tells everyone that she's never been married. Bernice Cooper lives right next to her and told me that Clara has men staying with her all the time. Ernie Hicks lived with her for nearly a year, and Bernice swears that Clara got an abortion while he was living with her. And Bernice said she saw Willard Hessler walk into Clara's bedroom, and he didn't have a stitch on."

"That must have been a sight," muttered Riley.

"You don't get it, do you?" she asked.

"Ah, she likes boys and not girls?"

"This is not a bit funny, Riley. The woman is a whore, plain and simple."

"Mother, we're simply going out to dinner," said Riley. "We're not swapping rings or anything."

"Of all the women in the world, and you pick Clara. Good Lord, what a match up, a virgin hooked up with a slut. Wonder how that will turn out."

"Two people going out on a date and having fun," said Riley. "That's how it will turn out."

"Probably get her pregnant."

"Ma, I don't know much about that kind of thing, but I don't think that Clara is…"

"Trust me, son," she said with a grave look on her face. "Women like her will do anything to nab you. They are sick and tired of working and want some man to support their lazy asses."

"Clara is not like that, Ma," said Riley. "She likes her job. I don't think she'd give it up even if she could."

Thelma slowly shook her head. "You're so naive," she muttered.

"Sometimes I can't believe you, Mother. You're putting down all females. You speak of them as if they were all devious by nature."

"They are, Son," she said pointing a finger at him. "They will do anything to get what they want. Why do you think this Clara would go out with the likes of you?"

Riley paused and lowered his head. "You know, Ma, I wouldn't expect to hear that from my worst enemy, let alone my own mother." He slowly opened the door and walked out of the house.

## Chapter Seven

Murphy was already sitting on one of the benches when Riley stopped in front of Lingo's Dry Goods Store. He got out of his truck and slowly ambled over to the bench across from Murphy.

"Where's dumb and dumber?" Riley asked.

Murphy smiled. "Well, I can see you're fitting right in with this bunch of misfits."

"Well, I figure the honeymoon is over. Time to get down to business."

Murphy glanced down Main Street. "I have no idea where those two are. They're usually here by now."

Riley cleared his throat; his face grew solemn. "Murphy, can I ask you a question?"

"Sure. Ask away."

Riley paused, then looked away. "Why do you think Clara wants to go out with me?"

"I don't know," said Murphy. "Why do you ask?"

"Well, we all know I wasn't the best looking kid in school. I'm just wondering if she has a motive for going out with me."

"What kind of motive could she possibly have? Murphy asked.

"Mother thinks she's after my money."

"Do you have any money?"

"Not much.

"Then I doubt that's the reason," said Murphy.

"That's why I'm asking," said Riley. "Because I can't imagine why anyone would agree to go out with me."

"You're being a bit hard on yourself, aren't you?"

"I don't think so," said Riley. "I'm just being honest with myself. I'm not very good looking, I'm as big as an ox, and I don't have much of a personality. Other than that, I'm quite a catch."

Murphy turned to face Riley. "In the first place, you're not that bad looking. The thing you don't understand about women is they don't judge men by their looks as much as we do when it comes to women. They're more concerned with personality and sense of humor. In fact, you could be Adolph Hitler himself, and as long as you can make a woman laugh, she'll think you're the greatest."

"But I don't even have a sense of humor," said Riley.

"Yes, you do," said Riley with a smile. "I've heard you crack a few funnies."

"Like what?"

Murphy paused as he looked away. "I don't know. I can't think of anything right now."

"There's a good reason for that," said Riley. "It's because I'm not funny."

"I don't know why you're kicking yourself in the ass," said Murphy. "Clara agreed to go out with you, didn't she?"

"Yeah."

"Then, what's all the fuss?"

"I just can't see why she agreed."

"Look, Riley," said Murphy shifting his weight. "Clara only wants two things from men, and she doesn't necessarily expect to get both things from one man…just one or the other."

"And just what are those two things?" Riley asked.

"She wants either sex or a few laughs, and if you're good enough to provide both, she'll probably go out with you a second time."

"Well, let's see," said Riley, scratching his head as he talked. "I'm not funny and I've never had sex. I'd bet money that this will be our only date."

Murphy looked up to see an old pickup truck stopping in front of them. "Here come Walt and Sully."

"Please don't say anything to Walter," said Riley.

"Wouldn't think of it," said Murphy with a quiet voice. He patted Riley on the shoulder. "Just go out with Clara and have a good time. Don't worry about it. Things will work out."

"What are you two yakking about?" asked Walter as he sat next to Murphy.

"We were just discussing what a good-looking guy you are," said Murphy.

"Now you sound like Sully," said Walter.

"Did someone mention my name?" asked Sully as he sat down as well.

"So, are you getting a little nervous, Riley, my boy?" asked Walter with a smile.

"About what?"

"You know what."

"Are you talking about my date with Clara?"

"Isn't it set for tomorrow night?"

"Six o'clock."

Walter leaned forward. "Planning on sticking it to her?"

"Huh?"

"Sex," shouted Walter. "Are you planning on having sex with her?"

"For God's sakes, Walter, I'm just going to…"

"You might wanna be careful. She's been having sex with just about every guy in town," said Walter holding back laughter. "You might want to wear a condom so as to keep things away from all of those wiener juices."

"Wiener juices?" said Sully. "You know, sometimes you say things that surprise even me."

"Look, guys," said Riley. "We're just going out on a date, probably out to dinner, maybe a movie. No big deal."

"Oh, for Christ's sakes, my friend," said Walter. "This is your big day. Don't blow it. You've never been laid, and you're going out with Clara Butts. Why do I see this golden opportunity standing right in front of you?"

"I just don't think it's right to try and take advantage of a woman on a first date," said Riley.

"Holy moly," said Walter. "Who's taking advantage of whom? This woman is always horny and hard up. She'll take even the likes of you. Don't mess this up."

Sully turned to Murphy. "You need to talk to Walter and make him shut up. He's embarrassing himself and he doesn't even know it."

Murphy cleared his throat. "Walter, I thought you were talking about taking Agnes out again."

"Oh, I've thought about it, but I just don't see a future in that gal. She's got bad hips, her boobs seemed to have disappeared, and she hasn't had sex in forty years. Hell, I doubt she can physically have sex. There's probably spider webs and moss growing down there."

"Good Lord," muttered Sully.

Murphy slowly shook his head. "Walter, when folks our age go out together, they have a tendency to socialize. Sex is the last thing on their agenda."

"Well, it's the first on mine," said Walter with conviction. "I'm not ready for the graveyard yet. If I can find a woman who doesn't mind looking at my saggy tits and wrinkly skin, I'm going to mount her."

"Now I'm dealing with an image that is going to give me nightmares," said Sully.

"How's Katherine?" Riley asked.

"Call her Kat," said Murphy. "That's all she's ever been known as."

"Is she doing any better?"

Everyone turned to Murphy with a solemn look.

"She's holding her own. Some days are better than others."

A silence fell on the group. Some looked away, and others kicked at the ground. Then, from around the corner, walked Gladys. She was smiling as she walked in front of the men.

Murphy nudged Walter. "Look who's out for a walk."

Walter looked up and smiled. "Hi, Gladys."

"Yeah, whatever, Walter," she said with a grim look and then turned to Sully with a smile. "Good morning, Sullivan."

"Sullivan?" muttered Riley.

"Well, good morning, Gladys," said Sully with a smile. "Out for a walk on this fine morning?"

"That I am," she replied, stopping in front of Sully. "Care to join me?"

"Maybe another day. Right now we're involved in high-level talks."

"Can't imagine them being too high if Walter is involved," she said.

"Maybe the next time?"

"It's a date," she said, then winked at Sully and marched off.

"Oh, you make me sick," said Walter.

"I think she was flirting with you, Sully," said Murphy.

"I'm about ready to upchuck," said Walter staring at the ground.

Sully watched her walk down the street, then turned to the others. "I really think she likes me."

"Give me a break," said Walter. "She's only trying to make me jealous."

"I'd say that was working for her," said Riley.

"That will be the day, when I'm jealous of a faggot like Sully here," said Walter with a touch of anger in his voice.

Sully smiled. “Well, you always said that any and all women are safe with me because I only like men. Here’s my chance to prove you wrong.”

“What do you mean?” asked Walter.

“If I date Gladys and end up having sex with her, will you finally acknowledge that I’m not a homosexual?”

“I most certainly will not. You are and always will be a flaming faggot.”

“But gays don’t have sex with women.”

“I don’t care. Nothing can change my mind.”

“Doesn’t matter,” said Sully. “I’m still going out with your ex-wife. It angers you, and that makes it all worthwhile.”

“Don’t do it, Sully,” said an angered Walter.

“You divorced her, Walt,” said Murphy. “She’s free to go out with whomever she wants.”

“Anybody but this gay bastard,” said Walter. “Besides, they’re both doing this just to piss me off.”

“Would seem that it’s working,” muttered Riley.

Murphy turned slowly to Sully. “All kidding aside. Are you really interested in Gladys, or is this just a means of getting back at Walter?”

“Oh, I’ve been attracted to Gladys ever since I’ve known her,” said Sully with a solemn look. I don’t know what she ever saw in Walter, but at least she came to her senses and divorced him.”

“I swear to God, Sully, I’m going to kick your ass if you don’t shut up,” said Walter.

“Can you feel the love?” asked Riley to no one in particular.

Murphy got to his feet. “I gotta go. I have too much going on at home right now,” he said walking towards his truck. “You guys battle it out, and I’ll see you tomorrow.”

As Murphy pulled into his driveway, he was shocked to see Lloyd’s car. Since he had already dropped off Emmy, Murphy did not expect to see him anytime in the near future. As he walked in the door, he found Lloyd standing near Katherine who was still in bed.

"Good morning, Son," said Murphy. "I wasn't expecting to see you so soon."

"Morning, Pop. I was dropping off a few of Emmy's things."

"So, what's going on?" asked Murphy. "You two look like you've been having a deep discussion."

Katherine shifted her weight and sat up in bed. "I was telling Lloyd about the man who was here last week and wanted to buy the farm."

Murphy frowned. "Oh, that guy."

"Dad, we were just discussing the fact that you have this golden opportunity to sell the farm," said Lloyd. "I know it's none of our business, but is it true that you refuse to sell?"

"That pretty much sums it up," said Murphy. "Why do you ask?"

"Pop, do you realize what a great opportunity this is? Farmland isn't exactly a great commodity right now. Prices are dropping everyday. If you have an offer, now is the time to sell."

Murphy took a seat near Katherine's bed. "Lloyd, pardon my asking, but why the sudden concern for my financial well-being?"

"I think we all know that I have no intention of keeping the farm after you and Mom are gone. I don't know anything about farming and could care less. Why not sell it now and get top dollar? It just makes sense."

"What you do with this farm after I'm gone is your business," said Murphy. "God knows there's nothing I can do about it after I'm gone, but until that time, there's no way that I would ever consider selling it."

"It's just a piece of land, Dad," said Lloyd. "That's all it is. If you're too old to work the land and we have no interest, sell it and turn it into cash."

"You know, I always dreamed that you would take an interest in the farm and that it would pass on to the next generation. This farm has been in the family for over a hundred and fifty years. There have been many Flemmings do many things to hang onto this farm. It has survived flood, fire, bad weather, and bank closures and is still owned by a Flemming. Generations of Flemmings have worked the land and managed to rear a family. Their blood, their sweat, and ultimately their bodies are buried in that soil nurturing it so that future generations can enjoy the same kind of life that it has always offered. All the generations that have come before have never considered it an inheritance.

It has always been more than just a piece of property. It has been a legacy passed from one generation to another. I consider it more than just a legacy. I think of it as a gift of love. It was a gift when my father gave it to me and a gift when his father passed it on to him. It's now approaching the end of the second century of being in the family and will soon be entrusted to you. The fate of the farm will rest on your shoulders. All I ask is that you do what you think is right. That's all. Whatever is the right thing to do should be your only concern."

There was a solemn silence. "Did you ever consider selling the farm, Dad?" asked Lloyd.

"Many times," he responded. "There were times I didn't think I was going to make it. Bad weather can kill an entire year's crop, you know. But the legacy had been passed onto me. It was my responsibility, and I was not going to disappoint the voices from the past."

"Voices? You heard voices?" asked Katherine.

"Indeed I did, as did all those who came before me. It may be the rustling leaves as a gentle wind blows through a field of corn or the lonely whippoorwill on a summer night. I can hear the echoes from the past when the midnight train rumbles over the Boggs Creek trestle, or the noises that this old house makes on a quiet night that sound like voices from the many graves of our ancestors of long ago.

"Yes, the voices are there, if you know where to listen. They haunted me, yet guided me to do the right thing. It will soon be your turn to do the right thing. If selling the farm should happen to be the right thing, then it will be your job to do just that. But don't ask me to do it for you. This land means more to me than any amount of money. You'll have to decide for yourselves when the time comes."

There was a strange silence that fell on the room. Lloyd felt uneasy, almost disrespectful from the comments he had made. He turned to his mother. "Where's Emmy?"

"I think she's in the barn," she replied.

"I need to talk to her," he said, heading for the backdoor.

Murphy followed him out onto the porch. He placed a hand on Lloyd's shoulder to get his attention. "Sit down, Son. I want to talk to you while we're alone." Lloyd said nothing. He took a seat on one half of the porch swing with Murphy on the other. Lloyd kicked the floor to put the swing in motion.

"Lloyd, I know this is none of my business, but what happened to your marriage? Is there anything you can do to save it?"

"I don't know, Pop. It just went sour. It wasn't as if it happened overnight, either. It was a gradual thing that seemed to sneak up on both of us."

Murphy leaned back in the swing. "There's an old expression that has to do with marriage. It seems so trite and simple that it seems hardly worth mentioning, but it has to do with working at a marriage. If you don't work at it and try to keep it fresh and alive, it will go sour."

"I can tell you from experience that happened to us," said Lloyd.

"Let me guess…the romance died."

"There's an old joke about why the woman was smiling when she walked down the aisle to get married," said Lloyd. "It's because she knows she'll never have to do that again. Well, Helen had a smile from ear-to-ear."

"Frustrating, isn't it?"

"Yes, it is," said Lloyd with conviction in his voice. "I don't think a woman could possibly know what the sexual drive is like for a young man. In time, I finally gave up on her. I didn't want to. I even tried to get her help. You know…professional help, but she refused. Then it seemed as if I lost respect for her. Sounds strange, doesn't it? Lose respect for someone because they won't make love with you. But I know that's what happened. It just seemed as if she didn't respect me or my feelings, so why should I respect hers? But that was just a stage I was going through. It was a transitional stage to where I am today. Yeah, I lost respect for Helen, but it was leading me to losing my love for her. Plain and simple, I fell out of love with her, and life is too short to live like that."

There was an awkward silence as Lloyd waited to hear his father's reaction.

"Well, that's all well and good for you, Son, but what do you think this divorce is going to do for Emmy?"

"It has to be better than listening to the fights and the…"

"No, don't you go down that road, Lloyd," said Murphy with a stern voice. "That's just an excuse that people use. There is no such thing as a kid wanting his parents to get a divorce. That's the last thing they want."

Lloyd grew silent as he stared at the floor. "I knew when we sat down here that you would make me see the hard truth. You've always taught me right from wrong even though I sometimes didn't want to hear it."

"Most of the time, the right way is the hardest road to travel," said Murphy.

Lloyd turned and leaned forward until he was only inches from his father's face. "Dad, do you remember when I was a little kid, and you bought me a BB gun? Do you remember that, Pop?"

Murphy smiled. "Sure, I remember," he said.

"God, I loved that gun," said Lloyd. "I was only about eight or nine years old as I recall and thought I was the toughest guy in the world, now that I was the proud owner of a BB gun.

"I remember that it was only a couple days after you gave me that gun that I was in back of the house shooting at just about anything in sight. I didn't know it at the time but you were watching me from a window when, suddenly, I began shooting at the birds sitting high up in the trees. I don't know whether I actually believed that I could hit one of them. They seemed so far off. Maybe, I thought of them as some kind of inanimate object. I don't know. All I know is that it wasn't long before I scored a direct hit, and to my surprise a bird began its descent from its perch, falling gracelessly as it bounced from one limb to another. I must say I was surprised. I never really thought that I would shoot one.

I remember that I walked over to the bird with a certain amount of apprehension. I wasn't sure if I should strut like some big game hunter after the kill, or cautiously creep up to the innocent little animal that I had needlessly destroyed.

I knelt beside the fallen bird, and with the end of my gun, I gently turned it over. From the colors on its breast, I knew that it was a female robin. I remember wishing that it was only stunned, and that it would suddenly awaken and fly away, but that was not to be. Her head dangled, lifelessly, to one side, and a small trickle of blood oozed from under her feathers and dripped onto the ground.

I nudged the bird with my gun hoping to arouse it from some deep sleep. Nothing. By now, the tears were flowing from my eyes as I finally came to realize what I had done. A sweet and innocent life had been taken, and it was my fault.

I don't know how long you had been standing beside me, but, suddenly, you were there bending down on one knee. You stayed there for the longest time. I remember that. I was dying inside. I felt so bad. I had done something very bad and deserved to be punished, and you calmly stared at the dead bird.

Finally, you turned to me and asked me if I understood what had happened here. I muttered something about an accident and how I'd never do it again and then you told me something that I never forgot. In fact, I'm sure that was your intention that it would be a day that I would remember all my life. You told me that today was the day that the life of a small bird ended. Hardly seems significant in the big scheme of things, but nonetheless, we have one less bird in the world today. Tomorrow, there will be one less song being sung by a creature whose only goal in life is to give happiness.

You, then, laid a hand on my shoulder, and when I finally worked up the nerve to look you in the eye, I noticed a tear falling down your cheek. To this day, I can't remember another time that I ever saw you cry. You told me that since God loves all life, even the lowly robin, and there must be a reason for this seemingly senseless death. It was then that you told me something that would guide my life from then on. You told me that, without doubt, God sacrificed that little bird so that I would learn a valuable lesson. I would be a better person after having seen how precious life is. Life must be preserved at all cost. Then, you told me that I should always remember the lesson that I learned so that the robin's dying would not be in vain. Do you remember that, Dad?"

Murphy was smiling as he stared out the window lost in rich memories of the past. He turned to face his son, his eyes twinkled. "You never shot any more birds, did you?"

Lloyd laughed. "I don't think I ever shot that BB gun again."

"I didn't expect you to turn into a sissy."

"Well, I knew I wouldn't be shooting any more birds. I couldn't stand the guilt."

"That's because you're a sissy," he said. Both men became quiet. They stared at each other, smiling with the knowledge that they had shared a memory and were now sharing a moment, a moment of peace and serenity that they had not known in years. Murphy took his son's hand and buried it within the safety of his own. "I love you, Son," he said with a smile.

"I love you too, Dad."

It was about that time that Belva swung open the door and stepped out onto the porch. She stared at the two men who were sitting close to each other and still holding hands.

“I don’t even want to know what’s going on out here,” she muttered.

Lloyd got to his feet. “I need to go find Emmy,” he said and started down the steps.

Belva turned to Murphy. “I heard you were whining the other day ‘cause I didn’t fix you no breakfast. Well, I fixed you breakfast today, and it’s on the table,” she said and disappeared back inside.

Murphy smiled with anticipation. He got to his feet and walked inside the house. As he turned the corner and entered the kitchen, his smile disappeared. There on the kitchen table was a bowl, a spoon, and a box of cereal.

Lloyd slowly stepped inside the open doorway to the barn. It was dark inside and the air was much cooler. He stopped to allow his eyes to adjust. He was surprised at how much the building had deteriorated. Sunlight streamed through the cracks in the siding revealing massive spider webs that seemed to cover the entire ceiling. The livestock stalls were empty now; most of them had been torn down.

Lloyd could hear whimpering and sobbing from the back of the building. He quietly crept to the back of the barn until he was standing over his daughter. She was sitting on a pile of hay, her face buried in her hands.

"Are you okay?" he asked.

"What do you think?" she replied as she wiped her eyes.

Lloyd eased himself down on the hay beside her. "Talk to me. What's wrong?"

"I think that should be obvious."

Lloyd scratched his head. "Well, I'm trying to decide if it's the divorce or living here with your grandparents."

"You're right on both counts," she said, blowing her nose on a tissue.

"I thought you liked staying here with your grandparents."

"I did before she got sick. They don't want me here, and I can't say as I blame them."

"You know they both love you."

"I know that, but that's not the point," she said. "They're going through a very rough time right now, and the last thing they need is a granddaughter hanging around."

"Actually, I was hoping you might be a blessing for them," said Lloyd rubbing his hands together. "I thought you might be a pleasant distraction."

"On top of that, I miss being home. I miss my room, my friends. It just seems as if my whole world is upside down, and it's your fault."

"Well, I never expected you to understand," said Lloyd. "This is something between your mother and me."

"She says you're an asshole."

"What?"

"Mother says you're a flaming asshole. I won't repeat the other names she calls you."

"I was hoping your mother would keep this between the two of us," said Lloyd. "You're smart enough to know that there are always two sides to every…"

"You know, I really don't care why you two can't stay together," said Emmy. "All I know is my life is down the shitter."

Lloyd smiled. "I'm not even going to say anything about the dirty word."

Emmy jumped to her feet. "You know what?" she barked. "I came out here to be alone, and you screwed even that up," she shouted and stormed off.

Lloyd watched her leave then slowly got to his feet. "Well, that went well," he muttered.

***

On the other side of town, Walter walked through the front door and into the kitchen carrying two bags of groceries. He set them down on the countertop and turned to Sully who was sitting at the table drinking coffee.

"When are you ever going to pay for some of the groceries around here?" Walter asked. "Or pay for anything for that matter?"

"I've told you many times that every penny of mine goes to your sister," said Sully sipping his coffee.

"Well, then, where do you plan on getting the money to take Gladys out on a date?"

"I was hoping you would loan me some money," said Sully.

Walter turned to face Sully. "You want me to give you money so that you can take out my ex-wife! Are you crazy?"

"Why? I'll pay you back."

"That's not the point," said Walter with a loud voice. "Don't you think that's asking a lot?"

"Look at it this way, if Gladys and I were to get married, I would be moving out of here," said Sully with a devilish smile. "Of course, I'd be moving in with her in your old house that she got from the divorce settlement."

Walter stared at Sully with rage in his eyes. "I swear to God there wouldn't be a jury in the world that would convict me."

Sully's smile got even bigger. "Somehow, that appeals to sense of order."

"Sense of order!" Walter barked. "How do you figure that?"

"You want me out of your life, and where do I end up? Still living in your house for free."

"Don't push me, Sully. I'm on the edge right now," he said as he poured himself a cup of coffee.

"Oh, by the way, your daughter, Casey, called while you were out," said Sully.

"And what did she want?" Walter asked as he sat down at the table.

"She wants you to go to church with her this Sunday."

"What the hell for?"

"Nice talk."

"Oh, get on with it," said Walter with a disgusted voice. "Why does she want me to go to church?"

"Your granddaughter, Rachel, is going to be singing in the choir."

"Oh, for Christ sakes."

"I would suggest that you get that potty-mouth under control," said Sully.

"Ah, I love my granddaughter, but I don't want to go to church."

"What's the big deal? I hear that a typical church service is only an hour."

"I don't know," said Walter with a frown. "I just don't feel comfortable in a church."

"Is it because you're a sinner?"

"Who's a sinner?"

"You're a sinner."

"I'm not a sinner."

"We're all sinners," said Sully. "My guess is the pastor himself can't make it through the week without committing a sin."

"Then why don't we all go to hell?"

"I don't know. Maybe, we do."

"So, if we're all going to hell anyhow, why don't we just have fun while we're here?"

"For goodness sakes, Walter. Some people ask God for forgiveness, and then they try to do better. These are what you might consider to be nice people who more than likely go to heaven, something you needn't worry about because the word, "nice" has probably never been used in a sentence with your name included."

"What makes you such an authority on religion?" Walter asked. "I don't see your sissy ass out the door on a Sunday morning."

"I'm not an authority," said Sully. "But I do read the Bible."

"I've never seen you reading the Bible," said Walter.

"I read it everyday."

Walter cocked his head and smiled. "Well, now, you're bound to go to hell because you're lying. I've never seen you read the Bible."

"I read it every night just before I go to sleep."

"Where do you keep the Bible?"

"Under my bed, not that it's any business of yours."

"Anything related to or near your bed is off limits to me," said Walter. "I can't imagine what goes on in there."

"So, tell me, why are you uncomfortable in church?" Sully asked in an effort to change the subject. "Is it because you're an atheist?"

"Well, I wouldn't say I'm an atheist," said Walter with a timid voice.

"Do you believe in God, or don't you?"

"I guess…kinda."

"Either you believe, or you don't," said Sully. "It's as simple as that."

"I just have a problem with believing that one guy can create all this stuff."

"Well, how do you think all this stuff came to be?"

"Huh?"

"Who created the earth, the people and the other stuff as you call it?" Sully asked. "And don't tell me we descended from the apes because I'll ask you why are there still apes."

Walter paused. "Quit backing me into a corner. I don't have all the answers."

"Bingo," said Sully. "None of us do. Nobody on earth understands these matters. We weren't given a brain that can comprehend such things. That's why we're told to have faith. You've been told that God did it all. Don't understand it? That's because you weren't meant to understand it. Have faith."

"So I suppose I should be going to church?"

"It wouldn't hurt," said Sully. "You might learn something, but I don't think that's the most important thing."

"Well, what is?"

"Talk to God. He wants to hear from you. He built you, loves even an idiot like you, and has plans for your life."

"He has a plan for my life?"

"Even a dumbass like you."

"How do I know what his plan is for me?"

"What do you like to do besides bitch about everything and everybody?"

Walter smiled sheepishly. "I ain't going to tell you."

"Why not?"

"Because you'll make fun of me."

"I probably will, but tell me anyway."

Walter paused, and then said, "I've always wanted to be a writer."

"There's nothing wrong with that," said Sully. "Chances are if you have the desire, you also have the talent. Have you ever written anything?"

"No."

"Why not?"

"I don't know," said Walter. "I just never tried, and now I'm too old."

"I don't know much about writing, Walter, but it would seem to me that age would be an asset. You've experienced things in your life that you wouldn't have had at an early age. The roads you've travelled in your life have given you a treasure of experiences and memories that will always be with you and are there waiting for you to use them by creating a story."

By that time, Walter was gazing at a blank wall. "Maybe you're right for once in your life."

"So, are you going to church this Sunday?"

"Sure. Why not?"

"Who knows? You might get an inspiration for a story," said Sully.

"Yeah," said Walter. "Who knows?"

# Chapter Eight

The next morning, Riley was the last to join the other three. He sat down on one of the two benches without saying a word. The other three were involved in small chatter pausing only to acknowledge Riley's arrival. There was a break in the conversation, and all eyes turned to Riley.

Walter smiled. "So, this is the big day, eh?"

"I don't know what you mean," said Riley his voice shaking.

"You know what I mean," said Walter. "Today is the day you go out on your first date."

"So, what?" asked Riley shifting his weight on the bench.

"So, what?" shouted Walter. "You're sixty-four going out on your first date, and you say, 'So, what?'"

"It's no big deal," said Riley. "We're just going out for dinner. That's all."

"You're going to piss her off," said Walter.

"What?"

"She's expecting to get laid, and if you let her down, she probably won't go out with you again."

"Jesus, don't listen to Walter," said Sully. "He knows nothing about women. Up until the time he got married, he still thought that every woman had a penis."

Riley leaned back nervously grabbing the bench. "I just don't think it's right to expect sex on a first date."

"Why not?" Walter asked. "She expects it."

"What if you're wrong?" Riley asked. "Wouldn't I look like a fool?"

"You probably will anyhow," said Walter.

By that time, Riley was fidgeting and didn't really hear Walter's remark.

"Let it go," said Murphy. "At least, he has a date. That's more than you can say."

Walter leaned forward. "You're scared, aren't you?"

"What?"

"You're scared of going out with Clara," said Walter. "Or with any other woman for that matter."

"I'm not scared," said Riley. "Just a little nervous."

"Give it a break," said Murphy. "Let's change the subject."

"You'd better get over that nervousness," said Walter. "You'll never get a boner if you're nervous."

"What?" Riley asked.

"It's a proven fact that a man can't get an erection when he's under stress," said Walter.

"Oh, good Lord," said Riley. "One more thing to worry about."

Murphy cleared his voice and got to his feet. "So, tell me, Walter. What's going on in your life?"

"Oh, you guys aren't going to believe this," said Walter. "I'm going to church this Sunday."

"You can't be serious," said Murphy.

"You remember my granddaughter, Rachel Gibbs, don't you?"

"Oh, yes," said Murphy. "Isn't she the cute one with the great sense of humor?"

"That's the one," said Walter.

"It's hard to believe that anyone related to you would be cute and funny," said Sully.

Walter flashed a cold look towards Sully then found his smile once again. "She's going to be singing in a kid's choir and wants me to come."

"Everyone else in the family must be out of town if she invited you," muttered Sully.

"She's a very talented young lady, and singing just happens to be one of her talents," said Walter with a look of pride.

"That's fantastic, Walter," said Murphy. "Hope you have a great time while you're there."

"I hope he learns something while he's there," muttered Sully.

"Sully," said Murphy. "What about you? What's going on in your world?"

Sully smiled. "I'm waiting on Gladys. We're going walking together."

"The only reason you're doing that is to piss me off," said Walter. "I can't believe you'd stoop that low, and then again I should expect this not only from a fruit cake like you but a slut like Gladys."

"Come on, Sully. It's time to confess," said Murphy. "Do you have a genuine interest in Gladys, or is this a means of getting back at Walter?"

"Oh, I think she's a real nice lady," said Sully.

"She's a whore," blurted Walter.

"For her age, she is very pretty with a great sense of humor and is extremely intelligent," said Sully.

"She's as ugly as a mud fence and dumber than a box of rocks," said Walter.

Sully turned and gave Walter a solemn stare. "Some people just don't appreciate women and their splendor."

"She's a cow, Sully," said Walter. "Not a woman -a cow."

"You're green with jealousy," said Sully.

"I am not jealous."

"Then, why are you saying such nasty things?"

Murphy sat back down. "Well, I can see how this day is going to go."

"So, how 'bout you, Murphy?" Riley asked. "How are things with you?"

Everyone turned to Murphy with a solemn look.

"Oh, we're taking it one day at a time," said Murphy with a sober voice.

"How's Kat doing?" Riley asked.

"She tells me that she's doing okay, but I know different."

"Is she getting any better?"

"There is no getting better," said Murphy. "It's all downhill from here on until…well, until the cancer finally wins."

"Must be tough," muttered Riley.

"Oh, yeah. It's tough alright," said Murphy staring blankly at the ground. "Every day I watch my soul mate, the woman I've adored nearly all my life, slip slowly away. There is no pain like this. I'd gladly give up an arm or a leg if I could have her back. The only positive thing I've learned from this is so simple and, yet, so mysteriously hidden from view is how important every day is. As each day passes, bringing me closer to losing her, I look back and decide if I got the most out of that day. Did I make her laugh? Did I laugh? Did I do something silly? Why not? Life is way too short to not enjoy every day. You think you're too dignified and sophisticated to do something silly? You're missing out if you do."

"Is she in pain, Murph?" Riley asked.

"No, thank God. She's taking medication. I would guess that takes care of the pain."

"How's her attitude?"

"A hell of a lot better than mine would be," said Murphy forcing a smile. "You'd think that nothing was wrong. She's her old cantankerous self. She's much braver than anyone I've ever known."

Riley cleared his throat. It was obvious that he felt uneasy asking questions. "What has the doctor said as far as how much time she has left?"

Murphy ran his fingers through his hair. "I don't know. One doctor said six months, and another said six days. I guess it's all up to God."

Sully leaned forward. "I think I speak for the others when I say if there is anything we can do…"

Murphy took a deep breath and sat up. "Sorry to bother you guys with this. The time we spend together on these two benches is meant for fun, not depressing news."

"What are you talking about?" Walter asked. "Every time Sully shows up is depressing."

Everyone laughed. It seemed to relieve the quiet tension.

Murphy got to his feet. "Well, I hate to cut this short, but I must be going." He started for his truck. "Take care, guys."

As Murphy walked through the backdoor, he could smell bacon in the air. He hung up his hat and entered the kitchen. Belva was scooping eggs out of a skillet and onto a plate.

"Want some breakfast?" she asked.

Murphy had a shocked look. "Sure."

"Sit down then," she said bringing the plate to the table. She then poured a cup of coffee and set it next to the plate.

"This is terrific," said Murphy taking a bite of the food.

"Don't get used to it," she grumbled. "That was going to my plate. You just happened to show up at the wrong time."

"Where's Emmy?" he asked between bites.

Belva poured herself a cup of coffee and sat down across from Murphy. "I don't know. She got up and headed for the barn. Spends most of time out there. Don't know why. Could be her way of getting away from all of us."

"Wish I had more time to deal with her," said Murphy sipping his coffee. "She's not too high on my priority list right now."

"Give me a week," said Belva. "I'll straighten her ass out."

"What would you do?" Murphy asked.

"Put her ass to work. The little bitch has been pampered all her life. She needs to know what it's like to be exhausted at the end of a day when there's no fight left in ya and all you want to do is to pass out on a bed. Any bed."

"I suppose you're right."

"Suppose? I know I'm right. One week, and I'll own her."

Murphy finished his food and leaned back with his coffee. "How's Kat?"

"Not good," she said rubbing her forehead.

"What's wrong?"

"I don't know. She seems so much weaker," said Belva. "You'll never see it. She puts up a front for you, so you won't worry."

"Should I call Doc Henson?"

"She won't hear of it. She doesn't want any more doctors."

"Should I call one anyway?"

Belva pointed to the doorway. "Go see for yourself."

Murphy slowly got to his feet. He felt reluctant to walk into Katherine's bedroom for fear of what he might see. It had been months since the terrible day when that seemingly uncaring doctor told him of Katherine's fate. The word, cancer, fell from his lips as if it were something as benign as a headache. The shock of that day was never forgotten nor had it diminished for Murphy. Each day brought small but discernable changes to Katherine, and as the weeks passed, the changes became more severe. She made a great and even heroic effort to hide the pain, but Murphy could sense that she was suffering. No matter what he offered to do to help ease the pain, she always refused, saying that she was just fine or that he was overreacting. Murphy knew better, but he also knew that it was best to just let it go.

He stepped lightly into her room. She was lying on her back with her eyes closed. Murphy stared at her for a moment then turned to leave.

"Where do you think you're going, old man?" she asked.

"Thought you were asleep," he said, turning back around.

"Just resting my eyes," she said, sitting up in bed. "Sit down and keep me company."

Murphy pulled a chair to the side of her bed. "How are you doing?"

"I'm fit as a fiddle and have no idea what I'm doing in this bed."

"The doc says that's the best place for you."

"Oh, what does he know? Has he ever had cancer? Good gracious no."

"I still think you should do what he says."

"Where's Belva?" she asked in an effort to change the subject.

"In the kitchen," he said. "She actually fed me breakfast. Well, kinda. It was supposed to be hers."

Katherine smiled. "Are you getting along with her?"

"As good as expected," he said. "She's not an easy person to get along with."

"Well, I like her and trust her to do the right thing."

There was a long pause as both thought about what to say next. Neither one wanted to bring up Katherine's health issue.

"We've had a lot of good years together," said Murphy with a warm smile.

"That we have," she said with the same smile.

"Any regrets?" Murphy asked.

"Oh, I don't know," she replied. "What about you?"

"Nothing that comes to mind," he said scratching his head. "I guess my biggest regret is not telling you every day how much I love you."

"Oh, I always knew that you loved me."

"That's not the point," he said. "A man should tell his wife every day how pretty she is and how much he loves her. I think it's important that a woman hear it every day."

Katherine took his hand in hers. "I never doubted your love for a moment." She reached into her pocket and pulled out a small cellophane bag. Inside was a lock of blond hair. "I do have one regret," she said as she handed it to Murphy.

He studied the bag for a moment then turned to her with a solemn look. "Becky?" he asked.

"I still miss her yet today," said Katherine.

"She was so young…not even three years old."

"I keep thinking there was a reason God took her from us at such a young age," said Katherine, returning the bag back to her pocket.

Murphy lightly patted her on the arm. "I'm just glad I got to spend my life with you."

Katherine closed her eyes for a moment then reopened them. "Sorry, Murphy," she mumbled. "For some reason I'm sleepy."

Murphy got to his feet. "You get some rest, and I'll see you later," he said and walked out the door.

Something didn't feel right to Murphy. He had known this woman nearly all his life, and there was something she wasn't telling him. His mind wandered as he tried to imagine what it was that she knew and wasn't telling him. Was her time nearly up, and somehow she knew? It was for certain she would not tell him if she knew, just to spare him the pain. For the first time in all the years he had known Kat, he felt emptiness deep inside. Murphy was scared. He was scared of losing the one thing in life that gave his life meaning. He was scared of losing the very heart of his soul and existence. It didn't seem fair.

Murphy wiped his eyes just before walking into the kitchen. Belva was still sitting at the table. He walked across the room and sat down across from her.

"So, what did you think?" she asked without looking up.

"Something's wrong," Murphy said as if in a daze.

"Why do you say that?"

"I don't know. I can just tell."

"What do you think is wrong?"

"I think she knows that she's going to die real soon," said Murphy.

"What makes you say that?"

"I've known that woman most of my life, and I know how she thinks and feels. Somehow, she knows."

"Well, I hope you're wrong," said Belva. "In the short time I've known that woman, I've become attached to her. Never could figure why she married the likes of you."

"Well, that's one thing we agree on," mumbled Murphy.

"If it makes you feel any better, I've seen many cancer victims, and quite a number of them were lucky enough to have their cancer stop. It defied everything the doctor predicted, but, nonetheless, they lived a normal life."

Murphy paused. "That's good to hear."

Belva turned and looked at Murphy. "By the way, you ain't done much around here since Katherine took sick, have you?"

The dazed look disappeared from Murphy's face. "What are you talking about?"

"Well, look around you. The place is a mess."

Murphy scanned the room. “It might need a little cleaning.”

“A little cleaning?” Belva asked. “It’s a damn good thing Katherine hasn’t been able to see the condition of this house.”

“I guess I can find some time to…”

Belva got to her feet and picked up dishes from the table. “You know, I don’t get paid for cleaning up after you folks, but I’m gonna give you a break, seeing as how you got enough on your mind. You just get on out of here, and I’ll take care of things.”

Murphy stood and watched her as she carried an armful of dishes to the sink. “I really appreciate what you are…”

“Never mind that,” she barked. “Just get out of the house while I clean things around here.”

Murphy walked across the kitchen and poured himself a drink of water at the sink. After gulping down its contents, he set the empty glass on the counter and gazed out the window at the backyard. He winced at what he saw. Trash littered the backyard, and the weeds grew wildly everywhere. Dried and peeling paint fell from the sides of the barn and garage, leaving white piles all around the perimeters of the buildings.

It wasn't always like that. There was a time when the stark white buildings stood proudly against the dark green grass. Murphy smiled as he remembered the smell of fresh paint and newly cut grass. Work clothes and flowered dresses hung from a clothesline that stretched the length of the backyard. In his mind, Murphy turned to watch his small children as they played on a tire hanging from an oak tree across the driveway.

"Murphy, supper's ready. Holler for the kids to come in."

Murphy turned and looked over his shoulder. "Right away, Kat," he said.

He walked onto the back porch and opened the back door. He stepped outside and looked in the direction of the oak tree. The rope and tire were gone. Even the branch that supported it had fallen during a storm years ago.

Murphy's face paled, and his smile disappeared. A gust of wind scattered the thin strands of hair on his head, and a discarded newspaper came to life, its pages spreading across the yard like ghosts in the wind.

"All those years ago," he muttered aloud, turning once again to the oak tree hoping to see that rope and tire. The fierce wind stung his tired eyes as Murphy gazed across an open field. He stared into a river of memories until his heart could no longer take it. "All those years ago," he said again and turned back into the house.

***

It was a little after five when Riley finished tying the knot in his new tie. He leaned forward into the mirror and straightened the knot. Stepping back, he took one last look at himself. The red and white striped tie looked good against the clean white shirt. He pulled on his sport coat and pulled down the raised collar. Since this was his first date, he wasn't quite sure how to dress, but he had learned over the years that it's much easier to dress down than it is to dress up. "Not bad," he muttered aloud.

"I wish you wouldn't go," said Thelma as she walked around the corner.

"That's enough, Ma," said Riley still staring into the mirror.

"You're going to be sorry."

"I'd rather go on a date and be sorry than to sit at home here another night," said Riley. "Besides. Who knows? I might get lucky."

Thelma covered her eyes with one hand. "I'm going to pretend I didn't hear that."

"You can pretend anything you want," said Riley. "I'm just getting tired of pretending that I will someday have sex with a woman."

Riley walked into the living room with his mother close behind. She sat in a rocking chair while he began to pace back and forth.

"I wonder if I should go now. It's after five," said Riley looking at his watch.

"Does she still live in that dreadful trailer?" Thelma asked.

Riley stopped and turned to his mother. "Trailers aren't dreadful."

"Hers is."

"It might need a little fixin' up."

"A little fixin' up? The junkyard is too good of a place for that thing. The last time I saw it, the door was open, and I saw a rat crawl up the steps and scurry inside."

"You saw a rat run inside Clara's trailer?"

"Yes, I did."

"Well, I'll bet you didn't see it run back outside," said Riley with a smile. "Knowing Clara, I'll bet I know what she had for dinner that night."

"Oh, good Lord," mumbled Thelma.

Riley began pacing the floor again. "How do I look, Ma?"

"You look nervous."

Riley stopped and turned to her. "I'm talking about my suit. How does it look?"

"It looks great," she replied. "Too bad it's out-of-style."

"What do you mean by that?"

"Nobody wears suits anymore. Kids today are lucky if they're even covered up."

Riley glanced at his watch again. "Wonder if I should go now. I think it's good manners to be early."

"You'll be lucky if she even remembered you two were going out," said Thelma.

Riley stopped and put his hands on his hips. "You know what's wrong with you? You're jealous."

"Jealous! Jealous of what?"

"You're jealous that there is another woman in my life besides you," said Riley pointing at her.

"Oh, good Lord," she said slowly shaking her head. "I can't believe you said that."

"Well, it's the truth."

Thelma snapped back and grabbed her head. "Oh, my goodness."

"What's wrong?"

"My head," she replied. "I have a sharp pain in my head."

"Oh, no, you don't," said Riley walking towards the front door.

"What?"

"You know what. You're trying to make me feel guilty and stay home," said Riley, opening the front door. "Well, it ain't going to work this time. I'm going out on my first date and you can't stop me."

"Oh, that's okay," she said, still grasping her forehead. "Don't worry about me. If anything should happen, I'll call one of the neighbors."

"You do that," he said and walked out the door.

It took Riley less than ten minutes to get across town. He turned down an alley and stopped in front of an older model house trailer. It was a faded yellow with cardboard covering the windows. At one end, supporting blocks had slipped, making the trailer rest at an angle. It looked as if the lawn had never been mowed. Weeds stood nearly four feet high with abandoned toys and furniture laying everywhere.

Riley found a trampled path through the weeds and walked carefully to the front door. Before he could even get his hand up to knock on the door, Clara swung the door open.

"Ain't nobody gonna sneak up on me," she said stepping aside. "I can see and hear everything there is up and down this alley. Come on in."

The steps were attached to the trailer, so when Riley climbed onto the first step, the entire trailer leaned his way. He froze.

"Oh, don't worry," she said turning away. "Even you couldn't tip this thing over. Come on in."

Riley stepped inside and closed the door behind him. His eyes went wide and his mouth gaped open as he slowly scanned the room. There were piles of magazines and newspapers stacked everywhere. Furniture and empty boxes were piled to the ceiling. Since the trailer was leaning to one end, many of the piles had shifted but were stopped by even more piles.

Out of the corner of his eye, Riley saw something move. He quickly turned to a pile of cardboard. He heard scratching near the top. By now, Riley was apprehensive wondering what kind of animal was making a scratching noise. Suddenly, a small kitten appeared. Riley smiled with relief. Then, as if the dinner bell sounded, a small herd of cats entered the room.

"Last count, there were twenty of 'em, give or take," said Clara.

Riley bent down to pet one of the cats. "Have you always loved cats?"

"Oh, I don't care much for them at all," she said. "It's just that some cats get the mange, and the owners turn them loose. I feel sorry for them and take them in. That one you're about to touch had such a bad case of it. He nearly died."

Riley jerked back his hand and stood upright.

"I noticed that one of the blocks slipped out making your…home lean to one end. Is that a problem?"

"Not really. Once all the stuff settled in its new home, we were good. Besides, it's good for the legs walking uphill."

Riley scanned the room once again. "You certainly have a lot of stuff."

"The neighbors call me a hoarder. Not sure what that means, but it must be bad."

Riley turned to the kitchen. "What is that metal thing in your kitchen?"

"Oh, that's a treadmill."

"You keep it in your kitchen?"

"Don't like gettin' on it all that much, so I just keep it in the kitchen. That way, whenever I want something to eat, I have to move the damn thing. I've lost fifty pounds since I put that thing in there."

Clara slowly spun in a circle as Riley glanced at her body.

"Lost fifty pounds, you say?" Riley asked.

"I know I have a few pounds to go," she said. "Working in a restaurant doesn't help much. I can tell you that."

"I can imagine…"

"So, what are we doing?" she asked. "Where are we going on our first date together?"

"Well, I don't want to be pushy, so I'll let you decide," said Riley.

"Let me decide? Good Lord, Riley, a real man doesn't let his date decide. He flat out tells her where they're going."

"Well, I was thinking about going to the diner for dinner then going bowling."

Clara frowned. "Well, for one thing, I don't like bowling, and for another, I hate eating at the diner. Let's go over to Prospect and eat at Abe's, then come back here afterwards."

"Whatever you say, Clara."

It was a short drive to Prospect. Not much was said. Clara would spot someone she knew and would ask if Riley knew that person as well. Riley spent the time wondering why Clara had instructed him to tell her where they were going, and then changed the plans almost before he had finished telling her.

Abe's was opened in the fifties as a hamburger joint catering to the lunch crowd. From the beginning he only had three things on the menu: hamburgers, French fries and baked beans. Sometime in the early nineties, he added coleslaw to the menu which was the talk of the town for months to follow. Then, a few years ago, with his son going off to college, Abe extended his hours to seven o'clock in the evening. Nothing else changed. It was still the same old four things on the menu. Surprisingly, his business increased. In fact, the sales in the latter part of the day soon exceeded the lunch business.

Riley parked in front of the restaurant and got out of his car. He waddled around to the other side and opened the door for Clara.

"Wow," she said. "Ain't nobody ever done that for me before."

"Men did that all the time back in the old days," said Riley. "I've seen it in old black and white movies."

"I wish other men like Wilber Bates would watch those same movies," she muttered.

Riley held the front door open for Clara and then pulled out a chair for her at one of the tables.

Clara smiled as she sat down at the table. "I believe I'm spoiled already. Keep watching those old movies, will ya?"

Riley sat down across from her. He began to strum his fingers on the table as he fidgeted in his chair.

"What are you so God-darned nervous about?" she asked with a look of concern.

Riley sat straight; his hands fell flush on the table. "I'm not nervous."

"Yes, you are."

"No, I'm not."

"You look as if you're waiting for the verdict from the jury," she said.

Riley strummed his fingers on the table again. "Well, I just…"

"Somebody told me this is your first date," said Clara. "Is that true?"

Riley glanced down at the table. "Well, when I was twelve, a young girl in the neighborhood came over and sat with me on the porch. We spent time on the backyard swings as well."

"Well, that ain't no date. I'm talking about when a guy takes a gal out to dinner and a movie. He then takes her out on some dark, lonely road and tries to boink her."

"I can't say as I ever…"

"Hell, when I was twelve, I'd already had sex with three or four guys. Even tried it with a girl. Didn't care much for that."

"That's quite a history of…"

"You seem a bit timid, if you don't mind my saying so," she said.

"I suppose it's because…"

"Have you always had a weight problem?"

It was about that time that a waitress stopped by and took their orders. As soon as she had left, Clara leaned forward with a smile.

"Are you still living with your mother?" she asked.

Riley paused. "Yes."

"Wow! That's really something," said Clara. "I don't think I ever heard of a man in his sixties still living with his mother. By the way, how is your mother?"

"She's fine."

"Was she excited about you going out on your first date?"

"Oh, I guess you could say that," said Riley.

"You don't sound very convincing."

"She has her moods."

"And I'll bet her mood on this was 'why is her boy dating such a slut as Clara,'" she said with a bit of anger in her voice.

"My mother has her own issues to deal with," said Riley.

"I know I shouldn't ask this, but have you ever thought about going on a diet?" she asked.

Riley began to laugh hysterically.

The smile on Clara's face disappeared. "What's so funny?"

"I know I shouldn't laugh at such a question, because you know nothing of my life and what I've been through."

"I take it you've been on a diet before."

"Practically my whole life," said Riley, wiping his eyes.

"Have you ever lost any weight?"

Riley leaned forward with a serious face. "I don't know whether you will believe this or not. Most people don't. Most people assume that all fat people are that way because they eat too much. They'd much rather believe that than the fact that some people are born this way. I think it makes them feel better about themselves. They think that I have self-control while this overweight person in front of me obviously has none. That's okay. If that's what it takes for them to feel good, then let it be me that they look at."

"Are you saying you were born that way?" she asked with a look of concern.

"I weighed over twelve pounds when I was born. Hell, the record is something like nineteen pounds."

"Your poor mother."

"When I was just a kid growing up, I tried everything. I ran every day and only ate scraps of food, but nothing worked."

"I'll bet the other kids made fun of you."

"Every day of my life as a kid. There was always someone wanting to beat me up. I only wish I knew why everyone hates fat people. It's not always our fault. Some of us are simply born this way.

"Wonder why?"

"A doctor once explained it this way. He told me to look around at this big ole world. Look at the variety of everything. There are a million different kinds of birds, bugs, animals in general. Then look at humans. There are no two just alike. He told me that God wanted variety in the world, a variety of everything including people, and that's why some are born fat. There's nothing I can do about it, so that's why I put up with the stares and the whispered jokes."

Clara paused. "Sorry, Riley."

"Oh, don't be sorry," he said. "There isn't much you could say that I haven't heard a million times."

It was about that time that the waitress delivered two plates of food to the table.

Riley picked up his napkin and covered his lap. "Since we've been sitting here, I've seen four different people steal looks at us, and I know they are asking themselves how did that fat guy ever get a date and how many plates of food will he eat? Well, so as not to disappoint them, let's eat."

It was nearly eight o'clock when they returned to Clara's trailer. By the time they had eaten their dinner, Riley had finally relaxed enough that he was laughing and joking with Clara. Now, as he sat down in her living room, his hands began to shake as he pondered his next move.

"Want a cup of coffee?" she asked.

"No."

"How 'bout a beer?"

"Yeah. I'll take one…a beer, that is."

Clara removed the cap from a bottle and handed it to him. "Damn! There you go again. Your hands are shaking again. What's wrong now?"

"Nothing. Not a thing."

"You're worried about what's going to happen next, aren't ya?"

"What do you mean?"

"You don't know how to get me in bed," she said with a smile. "And right now, shit is racing through your head as you try figure out what to do."

Riley wiped sweat from his forehead. "Well I'm not really…"

"Come on," she said grabbing his hand. "Let's go into the bedroom."

Clara led Riley into the bedroom. She let go of his hand as he sat on a wooden chair, and she sat on the side of the bed.

"We have to relax you," she said. "You're as nervous as a black guy at a Ku Klux Klan meeting."

Riley slumped a bit and leaned back on his hands.

"Know any jokes?" she asked.

"Huh?"

"Do you know any jokes?"

"Why?"

"To relax you by telling me a joke."

Riley turned to the ceiling. He paused for several moments.

"Wanna hear a joke from me?" Clara asked.

"Sure."

Clara shifted her weight several times on the bed as she prepared to tell her joke. "This guy picks up a chick and takes her home. They make love all night long, and in the morning he is lying there while she massages his…you know…his testicles. The guy says that it feels great but why are you doing that? She replies that since the operation she's been missing hers."

Riley doesn't budge. He doesn't even crack a smile.

"Get it?" Clara asked. "Since the operation she had been missing her own balls. Damn. That didn't even faze you, and it's one of my best."

"I got it," he said. "It was funny."

Clara stared at Riley for a moment as she tried to think of her next move. "I know an ice breaker. Let's get naked and get into bed."

Riley's face turned pale. He slowly turned and watched as Clara began to disrobe. She slowly unbuttoned her blouse, took it off and threw it on the floor. Then, as she reached behind her back to unsnap her bra, Riley jumped to his feet and announced, "I've got to go." With that, he ran outside, got in his vehicle and drove away.

# Chapter Nine

Walter and Sully were already sitting on one of the benches when Murphy sat down across from them. Murphy frowned as he studied the two men. They were sitting with their backs facing each other and both were sporting disgruntled looks.

"What's the matter with you two?" Murphy asked.

"Other than the fact that Sully here is a dumbass, not a thing," said Walter.

"Who's the dumbass here?" Sully proposed. "You're the one who wants to take Agnes out on a date."

"What's wrong with that?" Walter asked.

"Agnes is a nice lady, and we all know what you're going to try to do to her."

"Since when have you given two shits for Agnes Dutton?"

"I don't want to see any nice old lady get raped," said Sully. "Assuming you can even get it up."

"What makes you think I'm going to rape her?"

"You're the one who is always talking about how you need to get laid."

"Well, that doesn't mean I'm going to rape her," said Walter.

"How else are you going to get any? She isn't going to give it up for an old turd like you."

Walter turned to Murphy. "See what I'm talking about? It's like being married all over again. There's always somebody in the house picking on me. Hell, he's worse than a woman."

"Is that all that's bothering you two?" Murphy asked.

"Sully here came up with this dumbass rape thing just to take the attention away from what I discovered," said Walter.

"And what would that be?" asked Murphy.

"I came home to find Mister Faggot here alone with Percy Sloan," said Walter turning to Sully.

"Are you talking about that guy out on Dry Lane Road?" Murphy asked.

"Yeah," said Walter. "The guy who moved here two years ago, and nobody ever sees. He's the guy who walks, talks and acts like a queer."

Sully leaned forward. "How would you know what he's like if nobody ever sees him?"

Murphy raised a hand as if he wanted to be heard. "What were Sully and Percy doing when you came home?"

Walter jumped back. "They were talking. I guess."

"Were they in the bedroom?"

"No. Actually, they were in the kitchen."

"Did they have their clothes on?"

"Well…yes."

Murphy leaned back. "Walter, that hardly proves anything."

"I don't need to prove anything," said Walter. "I know two faggots when I hear and see them, and these two were flaming. They must let it all hang out when they get around someone of their own kind, because I never heard this one sound that bad."

"Morning, guys," said Riley.

The three men turned to see their fourth member of the geezer bench.

"Well, if it isn't Romeo," said Murphy with a smile.

"Did you have a good time on your first date?" Sully asked.

"Did you get laid?" Walter asked.

"Yes, I had a good time," said Riley taking a seat next to Murphy. "And I don't kiss and tell."

"I didn't ask you if you kissed her," said Walter. "Did you at least get to first base? I mean after all we're talking about Clara here."

"We're not teenagers here," said Riley. "I can't discuss things like that."

"Wow!" shouted Walter. "You hit a home run! I never would have believed it! You nailed Clara Butts!"

"Now, just a minute," said Riley with a smile. "I can't say…"

It was about that time that an older Ford sped around the corner and stopped in front of the men. It was Clara. She rolled down the window and left the engine running.

"I knew I'd find you here, Riley Hoagland," she shouted in anger. "I can't believe you left me standing there. I was taking off my clothes, and you ran off without so much as a go-to-hell. You're an asshole, Riley. Don't you ever show your fat face in my neighborhood again."

Having said that, she rolled up the window and sped away.

There was a long and awkward silence. Riley's face paled. He leaned back against the bench.

"I should have known," Walter muttered.

"Should have known what?" Riley asked.

"I should have known you would lie about last night."

"Lie! I didn't lie. You were the one who assumed I had sex with her."

"You didn't deny it."

"You never gave me a chance."

"You did the right thing," said Murphy with a loud voice. "And I know why you did it."

"You do?" Riley asked.

"With all the men that she's had sex with, why would anybody in his right mind would want to take a chance on getting some kind of disease?"

"Not me," blurted Riley with a smile. "No sir. I wouldn't want to take a chance."

Riley and Murphy shared a warm smile, a smile that was meant to say how grateful Riley was.

"How's Kat, Murph?" Walter asked.

"I'm not real sure," said Murphy getting to his feet. "I know I'm always cutting it short, but I need to get home. See you guys tomorrow."

***

It was late morning when Belva stepped into Katherine's bedroom. She set neatly folded towels on a desk then turned to Katherine. Something was wrong. She could sense it. Besides, she was lying flat on her back when she normally would be sitting up. Belva walked to her bedside and leaned over. Katherine opened her eyes and smiled.

"Are you feeling okay, Katherine?"

"Why don't you call me Kat like everyone else does?"

"I got too much respect for you."

"You're pretty mean to the others around here," said Katherine.

Belva patted wrinkles from the sheet with her hand. "That's because they're all just pawns in the game of life. You be the queen."

Katherine's smile turned warm and tender. "Have you got a minute?" she asked.

"Sure, Miss Katherine," Belva replied. "What's on your mind?"

"Have a seat," said Katherine patting the bed.

Belva carefully sat on the edge of the bed and turned to Katherine. "Must have something important on your mind. You ain't never asked me to sit down before."

"Well, I've got something I want talk to you about, and this seems to be as good a time as any."

"Fire away, Miss Katherine."

"I've only known you for a short time, but I somehow feel close to you," said Katherine. "I know what I'm about to ask you is a lot, considering we hardly know each other."

"You can ask me anything you want," said Belva.

Katherine paused. The smile disappeared from her face. "I know deep in my heart that I don't have much time left."

"Oh, you gonna be just fine," said Belva with a reassuring voice. "You gonna live to be…"

"No, Belva. You don't understand. My time is almost up. I can't tell you how I know it. I just do."

Belva paused. "Well, now, the Lord must have a reason for letting you know that your time is up. I'd rather think that your imagination is…"

Katherine reached over and took Belva's hand and held it tightly. "I want you to stay here and take care of Murphy."

"What?"

"I know it's asking a lot, but I want to know that someone is caring for him."

"Well, I don't know," said Belva. "I'm sure that once you're gone, he's gonna want me gone."

"Well, I thought about that. You're going to have to tell him that you have nowhere to go. Make up something about where you live and ask him if you can stay with him for a while."

"I gotta tell ya, Miss Katherine," said Belva. "I don't know your husband as well as you do, but my guess is he's going to want to be alone after you're gone."

"That's another reason I want you with him. I'm afraid he'll become some kind of a hermit. He'll isolate himself from the rest of the world. I just know he will."

"No disrespect," said Belva. "But how bad could that be? This is a crazy old world, if you ask me."

"I don't want him to go there," said Katherine. "He needs to be with others. If he should become a hermit, I'm afraid he wouldn't live much longer."

"Well…if that's what you want."

Katherine gripped her hand even harder. "Do you promise me?"

Belva smiled. "Sure. I promise. Now, why don't you get some sleep?" She backed out of the room and closed the door. As she returned to the kitchen, she glanced out the window and just in time to see Emmy toss a rock at the dog. She rushed to the backdoor and opened it.

"Emmy, get your scrawny ass in here," she shouted.

The young teenager folded her arms across her chest and scowled.

"I'll beat your ass if you don't get in here, and I mean right now!"

The young girl put down her head and walked across the backyard to the porch.

Belva pointed at the porch swing. "Sit down."

Emmy took a seat and folded her arms across her chest again. "Who do you think you are ordering me around like that?"

"Who do I think I am?" said Belva. "I'm your Lord and master, and I'm about to send you to hell."

"You can't talk to me that way."

"The days of you being a little shit are over. From now on, you will call me Miss Burke, and if I ever hear you backtalk your grandparents again, I will beat your ass. Your grandparents don't have time for your nonsense, so from now on you report to me. The days of you hanging around the barn doing nothing are over as well. From now on, I will have a work list for you to do. You are a spoiled little brat, and it's time you grew up."

"What are you going to do if I refuse?" Emmy asked.

"One of two things," said Belva. She turned and pointed at a slim board leaning against the wall. "I'll either break that board over your ass or send you back to your folks. I will not allow you to disrupt this family any more."

"I still don't see why you are making such a big deal out of this," said Emmy.

Belva sat down on the swing beside Emmy. She reached for Emmy's hands and she jerked them away. Belva grabbed them and held them tightly.

"I don't expect you to understand this because you're young and probably the most self-centered person I've ever known, but here it goes any way. Those two wonderful people have been together for over a half of a century. They raised kids of their own and sent them on their way. They've been through bad times and good. They spent years loving and taking care of each other, and now one of them is going to die very soon."

Emmy's eyes turned to Belva. "Grandma? How soon?"

Belva looked her in the eyes. "Anytime now."

"Oh," said Emmy with a shocked look.

"Can you see how devastating this will be for your grandpa? Can you see how much he's going to miss her? They've been together nearly all their lives. This is serious stuff, and it's no time for you being a problem."

Emmy paused as she stared blankly at the floor. "I'm sorry," she mumbled.

"What did you say?"

"I said I'm sorry and will try to behave."

"There ain't no try to behave involved here," said Belva. "You will behave, and right now, you've got dishes to do."

***

Riley opened the backdoor of his house and quietly stepped inside. He stopped and listened for any signs of his mother. He soon heard a groaning coming from her bedroom. He rolled his eyes as he slowly walked to her room.

"How are you doing, Ma?" he asked.

She slowly turned her head and glanced at him then turned it back. "Oh, I'll be okay."

"No, really, Ma. Are you okay?"

"Oh, I'll live. It's just the pain."

"Where's the pain?"

"All over."

"Want me to go get the doc?"

"Oh, no. I'll be fine. You just go see to your girlfriend."

"Oh, so that's it."

"What are you talking about?"

"I go out on my first date, and you become sick. I think you're jealous."

"Of whom?"

"I think you're jealous that I had a date with Clara."

"You've got to be kidding me," she said. "You think I'm jealous of that pig?"

"She's not a pig."

"Oh, yes, she is."

"Isn't it strange how all of a sudden you're no longer in pain?" asked Riley.

"What are you talking about?"

"When I first came in here, you were in pain all over."

Thelma grabbed her head. "Oh, I'm still in pain."

Riley smiled. "Yeah, that's what I thought."

"Are you going to go out with that Butts girl again?"

Riley blushed. "Don't really know. Clara is not too happy with me right now. I'm sure you'll be pleased to know that she doesn't want anything to do with me."

Thelma smiled. "Why? What happened?"

"I'd rather not say," said Riley. "But she's rather upset with me right now."

"The only thing I can think of to cause that whore to be upset is for you to refuse to have sex with her."

Riley shook his head. "I just don't want to talk about it right now."

"I'm so proud of you, Son. You refused to have sex with the tramp."

"I didn't refuse," he said. "I…I got scared."

"Whatever the reason, I'm just so happy you didn't fall into her trap."

"What are you talking about?"

"Every woman dreams of trapping a man," she said. "Once they give you what you want, they own you."

"Ma, how can you say such a thing? You make it sound as if women are evil."

"Trust me on this one, Son. Once you cross that line, they've got 'cha. It's just a good thing you're done with her."

"Oh, I'm not done with her," said Riley.

"But I thought you said…"

"It doesn't matter what happened before. I'm going to win her back."

Thelma grabbed her head. "Oh, the pain. I swear I hurt all over."

***

It was late afternoon when Murphy got home. He was tired and a bit depressed, but he shook it off before entering the house. He was convinced that the last thing Katherine needed was a husband in a bad mood. He opened the backdoor and froze at what he saw. Emmy was standing in front of the kitchen sink with her arms buried in dish water.

"What in the world are you doing?" he asked.

"I'm washing the dishes, Grandpa," she replied. "I just finished sweeping the porch and doing a load of clothes."

Murphy said nothing. He simply stared at his granddaughter with an open mouth. "Are you okay?"

Emmy pulled out a bowl, rinsed it and set it in the drainer. "I'm fine. Why?"

It was about that time that Belva entered the kitchen. She glanced at Emmy and then at Murphy.

"Did you have anything to do with this?" Murphy asked.

"Emmy and I had a talk, and she agreed that it was about time she helped out around here."

Murphy stared at Belva for several moments and then turned to his granddaughter.

"We're going to start dinner in a while," said Emmy. "We're having meatloaf."

"Good Lord," he muttered. He then turned back to Belva. "Is Kat awake?"

"As far as I know," said Belva.

"How is she doing?"

"Not too good," she replied. "She's talking crazy. Talking about dying. I can't say as I remember a time when…"

"I need to be alone with Katherine," said Murphy as he started for the door. Please don't let anybody in there."

Murphy walked down the hallway and quietly opened her bedroom door. She was lying on her back staring blankly at the ceiling.

"Are you okay?" Murphy asked.

Katherine slightly lifted her head then returned it to the bed. "Murphy, you're just in time."

"In time for what?"

"I…I can't really say."

"What do you mean by that?"

"I promised I would not tell."

"You promised whom, and what did you promise?"

Katherine lifted herself up and leaned on her elbows. "It's time, Murphy."

"What do you mean it's time?"

"I was granted a few minutes to say goodbye to you, and that's why I was so happy to see you.

"Lady, you're talking in riddles," said Murphy. "Who was it that granted you the time?"

Katherine turned away. "Murphy, would you please open that window over there?"

"Sure," he said as he walked across the room and opened the window only to hear music playing. "Where is that music coming from?"

"It's coming from the record player in the living room," she replied.

"Who started it? You certainly didn't."

"Recognize the tune?" she asked.

"Why, of course," said Murphy. "That's Rachmaninoff's Rhapsody on a Theme of Paganini. That's our tune."

"Remember? It played on the radio on our first date."

"How could I ever forget," he said with a warm smile. "I never grow tired of hearing that music. Remember when the movie *Somewhere in Time* came out? I bought the soundtrack and actually played it so many times, I wore it out. I had to go buy another one."

Katherine smiled. "As I recall, you wore that one out as well."

The smile on Murphy's face disappeared, his face saddened. He slowly walked over to the bed and leaned over until his face was only inches from hers. He had regretfully thought about this moment for most of his life. It was a nightmare that he knew for certain he would someday visit, and here it was. "You know, don't you?" he whispered.

She stared at him with the same loving eyes that had graced him for over fifty years. “Yes,” she replied with a voice soft enough that only Murphy could hear.

Murphy’s heart was breaking. “God was here, wasn’t He?”

The smile on Katherine’s face broadened. “He’s still here.”

Murphy couldn’t hold back the tears any longer. He stood straight and leaned his face into his folded hands. “Please don’t take this soul away from me. I beg you. I will do anything…anything just to have her even one more day. Please, God, don’t do this. This dear, sweet woman is the core of my very existence. I can’t live without her.”

Murphy wiped his eyes and turned to Katherine. Her smile was gone, and her eyes were wide as if she had been jolted by something unseen.

“Good bye, Murphy,” she said, her voice fading, and her eyes closing. “I love you.”

“No, please don’t do this,” screamed Murphy. He bent down and scooped her into his arms. As he held her close, he heard her last breath and felt it against his skin. He held her tightly for a long time after she was gone remembering the good years and the younger years when they both had the whole world ahead of them. It was a better time, a time for embracing the future and not the past.

Murphy softly returned her to her bed and stood up. He wiped his eyes as he stared at her aged but beautiful face. “Good bye, my sweet. I love you too.”

# Chapter Ten

The funeral and the gathering afterwards were unbearable for Murphy. Close friends and kin whispered condolences into deaf ears. He blindly responded with words of gratitude, but his mind was somewhere else. He had often wondered what these days would be like and had anticipated a very depressing time, but he had never expected this much pain. He knew that his friends meant well, but the truth was he just wanted to be left alone. The guys down at the geezer bench didn't expect him the first day or two, but when the days lapsed into weeks, they became concerned. They talked about paying Murphy a visit but decided against it. Everyone in town knew that Murphy wanted to be left alone, and out of deep respect for the man, no one came to his house.

It was a bright and sunny morning. Murphy came in through the backdoor after completing a few daily chores to find Belva standing at the stove.

"I got ham and eggs here," she said.

Murphy stopped and stared blankly at the wall as if he were in deep thought. "Not hungry."

"Mr. Flemming, you needs to eat."

"Still not hungry."

"I can't remember the last time you had anything for breakfast," Belva said with a concerned voice.

Murphy pulled out a chair. "Sit down, Belva. I need to ask you something."

With a look of shock, Belva walked over and took a seat. "What did I do wrong?"

"Not a thing, Belva," said Murphy. "I just wanted to ask you something. You've been here for quite some time, and I have to tell you that I've appreciated your help. I'm not real sure what I would have done without you, but I have to ask you why are you still here? You came here because of Katherine's illness and now she's gone. I would say that your work here is finished."

Belva smiled. "Oh, Mr. Flemming, I've seen what you're like in the kitchen. I'm not real sure you could fix a bowl of cereal, and I damn sure know you have no idea where the clothes washer even is."

"Well, I appreciate your thoughtfulness, but I'll get along," said Murphy. "Besides, you probably need to get back to your family."

"Oh, you see. That's just it. I ain't got no family anymore. They all growed up and left me by myself."

"What about your husband?"

"He done left too. Says he went and found someone a lot nicer than me."

"What about your house?"

"We were just renting a place over by the railroad," said Belva. "Somebody else is living there now. I was wondering if you'd mind terribly if I stayed here a while. I got no place to go right now, but I'll figure something out. Would that be okay, Mr. Flemming?"

Murphy grimaced while he thought about what she had said. "Well, just for a little while."

"Not a problem," said Belva. "I'll be moving on as soon as I can find a place."

"And don't call me Mr. Flemming. That sounds like my father. Call me Murph."

"Yes, sir, Mr. Flemming…I mean Murph."

"And don't treat me so nice anymore. The funeral is over, and you can go back to your grumpy old self."

"Damn! Best news I've had in a while," said Belva. "Now do you want some eggs and ham or not? I ain't got all day."

After finishing his first breakfast in over a week, Murphy entered his bedroom where he had been spending all of his time since Katherine's death. He turned on the television just to give the appearance that he was actually watching it. He then settled back into his rocking chair, lost in a world of memories.

It seemed like only yesterday when he first met Katherine. She belonged to a new family who had just moved in not too far from the Flemming farm.

It was the summer before Murphy's last year of high school. As it was with all farmers' sons, Murphy spent his days working the land at his father's side. This was the natural order of things. It was the training and the preparation of the young man for the day when he would follow in the footsteps of his father and his father's father and assume control of the operation of the family farm.

It had been a week since the new family had moved into the farm next to theirs when Murphy's mother summoned him to the kitchen. She handed him a just-out-of-the-oven apple pie and ordered him to deliver it to the new neighbors as an effort to make them feel welcome. Murphy protested for the inconvenience but reluctantly grabbed the dessert and started down the road. It was a short trip less than a half mile, and it was no time at all until he leaped onto the front porch and knocked on the screen door. He heard footsteps and the screech of the screen door.

Murphy's eyes widened and his mouth dropped open. Before him stood a young woman of seventeen with auburn hair that flowed over her shoulders like the finest silk and eyes that sparkled blue radiance.

"Hi, I got pie," he blurted.

Katherine smiled. "I can see that," she said. "Is there some reason you came all the way over here to tell me that?"

"Huh?"

"Why are you standing on my front porch with one thumb stuck in what appears to be a homemade pie?"

Murphy closed his mouth and glanced down at his hand. "Oh, my God!" he muttered. "I'm so sorry!"

"That's okay," she said with a smile.

Murphy paused as he stared at the young woman. "My mother wanted you to have this because you're new. I mean you came here from somewhere else. Of course, you knew that, and so did I." He frowned at what he had just said.

"Here," he blurted as he thrust the pie in her direction.

"Thanks," she said with a startled look.

"I'll see you again," he said putting his hands on his hips and then dropping them to his sides. "I have to go since all I came here for was to give that to you, not that I didn't enjoy meeting you, but I think I should go now," he said as he turned and jumped off the porch.

He was nearly halfway home when he stopped and turned around. She was still standing on the porch looking in his direction. He could see her soft hair as it waved melodically in the gentle wind, her dress dancing at her knees. "I'm going to marry that girl someday," he said aloud. "She will be my wife."

Murphy leaned back in the chair and fell asleep.

***

It was nearly eleven o'clock in the morning when Thelma Hoagland got out of bed. It was nearly lunchtime, and she guessed that Riley would soon be getting hungry. She put on her bathrobe and slippers and trudged into the kitchen. She was halfway across the room when she turned and saw her son sitting at the table drinking beer.

"What in God's name are you doing?" she shouted.

Riley upended his bottle and slammed it on the table. "What does it look like I'm doing?"

"Well, excuse me for asking, but I've never seen you drink alcohol before."

The kitchen table was covered with about as many empty bottles as there were full ones. Riley knocked an empty one over reaching for a full one. He popped the cap off and gulped from the bottle. "Well, there's a first time for everything."

She walked over to the table. "Why, out of the clear blue sky, are you doing this?"

Riley kicked out the chair next to him and pointed at it. "Sit down, Ma. Take a load off."

With great caution, she sat down and scooted the chair away from him. "I've never seen you act like this," she said with a shudder.

"Look at me, Ma," he said with his arms opened wide. "I'm pathetic. How many men do you know my age that are still living with their mother?"

"Well, there was that one man who lived…"

"Look at me, Ma. Look at me just once for who I am. Most men my age are sitting back, retired from a good-paying job, been married most of their lives and enjoying their grandchildren. That's a life, Ma. That's a real life. Do you know what it's like to go to a restaurant by yourself? You sit there and watch couples laughing and having a good time. They sometimes lean over and kiss each other. Do you know how much I've wanted that?"

"Well, son, there are a lot of people in this world who never get married. In fact, that seems to be the new trend."

"But they choose that way of life. That's the way they want to live. I don't. I want a wife, kids and a house. I want to be a part of the American dream. But here I am. I'm an old man living with his mother. The saddest part of all is I finally get a woman to go out on a date with me which is about fifty years late, and I screw that up. Good Lord, what do I do now? We both know I can't wait another fifty years to find someone. Most of my life is over, Ma, and now when I look back I feel as if I wasted it. What good did I do? Most people have a talent they pursue and eventually make a contribution of some sort. For some, it comes naturally. Then there are others who have to work at it for years to perfect their talent. Me? I have nothing to contribute to society. When I die, I will leave nothing behind to show I was here, not even a son to carry on the name."

Thelma moved closer and took Riley's hand. She had seen him in a depressed mood before but nothing like this. She felt so sorry for him, but there was nothing she could do. He was her only child and unfortunately took after his father who had been grossly overweight and very much a loner. She sometimes wished that she had never had Riley, and if she had known he would be just like his father, she would have given him up.

"Riley, you're beating yourself up for no reason," she said with a pleading voice. Billions of people have come and gone, but there's only one Shakespeare. There was only one Abe Lincoln and one Walt Disney. What I'm trying to say to you is, we were put here on earth to live as good a life as we can. The only real requirement is to do as much for others as you do for yourself. It might just be a kind word or a joke when someone is feeling down. God doesn't expect us to change the world. He only wants us to try to help our neighbors in a way that makes their lives a bit better. You're expecting too much out of yourself."

"Ma, I don't think you get it," said Riley. "I'm not looking to be the CEO of some big company. All I want is to have someone to love. That's all. You wouldn't think that would be such a big deal, but, obviously, it is for me."

"Maybe you're too picky," she said.

"Too picky? Is that what you said?" Riley asked. "The only date I've ever had was Clara Butts, and you call me too picky?"

"You're just going to have to be patient and wait for Miss Right to come along," she said.

"It took me sixty-five years to find Clara and you want me to wait for Miss Right? I don't think so. I'm going to do whatever it takes to win back Clara."

Thelma leaned back and grabbed her head with both hands. "Oh, my, does my head ever hurt."

"Imagine that," said Riley.

***

The next morning brought dark gray clouds that rolled ominously across the sky. Riley got out of his truck and gazed up at the sky as he walked over to the bench.

"Looks as if we're going to get rained out," said Riley as he took a seat.

"That's okay with me," said Walter. "I got shit to do."

"Have either of you heard from Murphy?" Riley asked.

"Not a thing," said Walter.

Sully cleared his throat. "Bernie over at the barbershop said that he heard Murphy stays in his bedroom all day long and never comes out."

Walter turned to Sully. "You do know that Bernie freely admits to be a homosexual, don't you?"

"Yes, I heard that."

"So what are you doing hanging around him?"

"I'm not hanging around him."

"Then how did you hear about Murphy?"

"I was in there getting a haircut."

"I don't doubt that you get one everyday," said Walter.

"How can you say things like that when you know where I'm moving?"

Riley turned to Sully. "Moving? Where are you moving to?"

Sully slowly turned to Walter with a smile. "I'm moving in with Gladys."

Riley turned to Walter, then back to Sully. "You're kidding me."

"Nope," said Sully. "It happens tomorrow."

"What about you, Walter?" Riley asked. "How do you feel about this?"

"I'm thrilled to death. Couldn't be happier. I've wanted to get rid of his ass for years now."

"It doesn't bother you that he's moving in with your ex-wife?"

"In the first place, he's doing this to try and prove that he is straight and not a faggot. I know there's no way he'll have sex with Gladys. In the second place, they deserve one another. They're both a pain in the ass."

Sully sat up straight. "How do you know I won't have sex with Gladys?"

"Well, for one thing, she isn't a man, and the other reason is you've never seen Gladys in the nude. If you can get it up after seeing that woman naked, more power to ya."

"You're just jealous," said Sully.

"Jealous? Jealous of what?"

"Because somewhere in the back of your mind, you realize that I'll soon be making love to your ex-wife," said Sully with a mischievous smile.

"I don't care if you bang her like a screen door in a hurricane," said Walter. "Just as long as I don't have to look at either one of you again."

"Has either one of you seen Clara?" Riley asked.

"I had breakfast at the diner, and she was working," said Walter. "Why? Changed your mind and want to see if you can get some of that?"

"Jesus, Walter," said Riley. "You sound just like a teenager."

"Finally!" said Sully. "Finally, someone sees what I put up with everyday."

"I thought you and Clara had parted ways," said Walter.

"I want to see if I can get another chance," said Riley. "After all, the women aren't exactly breaking down my door trying to get at me."

"I don't doubt that," Walter mumbled.

"What did you say?" Riley asked.

"I said you could do worse than Clara."

"Really? Who would be worse than Clara Butts?"

"Well, you could be dating Janice Dix," said Walter. "There are those who think she's a guy who had an operation."

"You're kidding me."

"You might ask Sully over here about that one," said Walter. "That sounds like someone in his perverted world."

Walter turned to Sully. "Hey, I don't even know a Janice Dix," said Sully.

Riley got to his feet. "Well, I gotta give it a try."

"Going down to the diner?" Walter asked.

"That's the plan."

"Well, good luck, ole buddy," said Walter. "By the way, pancakes is the special of the day."

"Thanks," said Riley and walked away.

The diner was only two blocks away, and Riley had it virtually to himself. It was too early for the lunch crowd and much too late for those wanting breakfast. He took a seat at the far end of the dining area nervously waiting for Clara to appear from the backroom.

Several minutes passed before she finally pushed through the swinging doors. She slowly scanned the room looking for customers, her eyes stopping on Riley. She frowned, then slowly walked over to his table.

"What are you doing here?" she asked.

"I just wanted to see you," he replied.

"That's funny. People who come in here want something to eat."

"Okay, I'll take a hamburger."

"Do you want anything to drink?"

"I'll have a coffee."

She turned to leave. "I'll be right back with your coffee."

Riley fidgeted with the salt and pepper shakers. She obviously had not forgiven him, and he was grossly embarrassed by what had happened. He scanned the room. There were two older couples at the other end of the diner, and he was quite certain that they had not noticed him. He thought about getting up and leaving, but he was afraid that would infuriate Clara even more than she already was.

Clara returned carrying a cup of coffee. She all but dropped it on the table and turned to leave.

Riley cleared his throat. "Clara, do you have a minute?"

She stopped then turned around. "One minute, and that's it."

"Can you sit down with me?"

"No. What do you want?"

Riley ran his hands through his hair. "I'm so sorry about the other night."

Clara maintained a frown and did not move.

"I should have known I would freeze like that," said Riley with a soft voice. "I've never been with a woman. I didn't know what to do. I seriously did not know what to do. I don't expect you to forgive me, just understand why I did what I did. I am so sorry, Clara."

She began to fidget with her hands and even forced a smile. "I guess I've had worse things happen to me. Can't remember just what it was."

Riley smiled. "Any chance we might try it again?"

Clara paused. "I'll think about it."

"Fair enough," said Riley.

"I'll be right back with your hamburger," she said and walked off.

***

It was early evening. The sun was just starting to show off its red and orange streaks of day-ending light. Murphy once again closed his bedroom door behind him and settled back down in his rocking chair. His mind soon drifted back to a time when his son, Lloyd, was just a little boy. As most young boys, Lloyd loved and had a great respect for all animals.

It was a hot and dry summer, hotter than any summer on record. The drought had lasted nearly a year with only an occasional light sprinkle of rain. Just like all of the other farmers in the area, Murphy was concerned for his crops. Losing his crops would be a financial disaster. Most of his time was spent loading water from his well into a large tank in the back of his truck. He then transported it out to his fields where he sprayed the crops.

Murphy had just returned from a short run and was filling the tank on his truck for another run. As he waited, Murphy noticed Lloyd quickly yet steadily walked around the corner of the house. He had his hands cupped together as he walked into the woods. He then returned to the back of the house and made the same trip into the woods.

Out of curiosity, Murphy sneaked across the yard to the other side of the house. He watched as the small boy returned to the back of the house. He turned on the spigot to allow a few drops of water to pool in the palm of his hand. He turned off the spigot, got to his feet and carefully walked back into the woods.

After watching this strange behavior for several minutes, Murphy decided to follow his son as he disappeared into the forest. There not ten feet inside stood six full-grown adult deer. Lloyd crept slowly to within a foot of them and bent down to the ground. Murphy was about to scream at him when he noticed something on the ground. It was a small newborn fawn. It slightly lifted its head as Lloyd bent down, and it lapped the small trickle of water from his hands.

Murphy looked up at the adult deer towering over his son. They were watching him with guarded attention, but strangely enough, they were allowing Lloyd to perform this act of kindness.

"All those years ago," muttered Murphy as he drifted off to sleep.

# Chapter Eleven

"Well, this is the day you've been waiting for," said Sully as he walked in from loading a box into the truck. "From now on, you'll have the house to yourself. Aren't you thrilled?"

"I cannot tell you how excited I am," said Walter with a stone face.

Sully stopped what he was doing. "You don't look excited. In fact, you look depressed."

"Why in the world would I ever be depressed over getting rid of you?"

Sully smiled. "Probably because you love me so much."

Walter poured himself a cup of coffee. "Coming from a faggot, that's scary."

"You'll soon change your mind about me when you catch Gladys and me in bed together," said Sully.

"Oh, good Lord," said Walter with a look of disgust. "I can't imagine which of you two would look the worst in the nude. I just hope I never find out."

Sully picked up some loose clothes and draped them over his arm. "Don't kid me. That's a fantasy of yours. You've wanted to see me naked for years."

The two men walked slowly across the room to the backdoor. Walter fidgeted as he stared at the floor. He glanced up at Sully but turned back to the floor.

"Hell, I remember the first day you showed up at my backdoor," said Walter. "I told you not to marry my sister."

"Well, it wasn't all her fault," said Sully. "I'm not the most agreeable person in the world."

"I won't argue with that," Walter muttered.

The two men grew silent. They began to fidget again. Suddenly, Sully reached up and wrapped his arms around Walter.

"Take care of yourself," said Sully.

Walter backed away. "You'll be back," he said. "Once you find out what a pain in the ass Gladys can be."

"You'd take me back?"

"We'll talk about it."

***

It was early afternoon of one of the hottest days of the summer. Riley walked in from mowing the lawn. He was dripping sweat as he walked across the floor so decided to take a shower.

Thelma rolled out of her bed and slowly walked into the living room. She was about to sit in her easy chair when the front doorbell rang. She opened the door to find Clara Butts.

"What do you want?" Thelma asked.

Clara peeked inside the door. "I wanna talk to Riley."

"He's busy."

"Doing what?"

"He's taking a shower."

"I'll wait."

"He takes a long time," said Thelma. "There's a lot there to wash."

"I don't care," she said as she stepped inside. "I'll wait." She then walked across the living room and sat on the couch.

Thelma stood motionless as she watched her sit down. "Come right on in. Don't let me stop you."

Clara scanned the room as she chewed her gum with her mouth open. "You've lived here all your life, haven't you?"

"Yeah."

"Wasn't this your parents' house?"

"Yeah. Why?"

"I was just wondering how you ever got such a place," said Clara. "You've never worked, have you?"

"I worked for a while down at the grocery store."

"When was that?"

"When I was in my twenties."

"Wow," said Clara. "That must have been back before electricity."

Thelma sneered. "What do you want with Riley, anyhow?"

"I kinda think that's our business."

"You come waltzing in my house, and uninvited, I might add, and you have the nerve to tell me it's none of my business?"

Clara scanned the room. "Don't you ever update this place?"

Thelma glanced around the room. "What are you talking about?"

"This place looks like it's from the dark ages."

Thelma set up straight in her chair. "Well, at least it ain't on wheels."

"Oh, are you referring to my trailer?" Clara asked.

"Who else has a house on wheels in this town?"

"Kinda makes you a bit jealous, doesn't it?"

"Jealous," said Thelma. "Living in one of those things just makes you trailer trash."

"Well, I'd rather be trailer trash than an old bitch like you," said Clara.

"I think you should go now."

"I know you have a tight grip on Riley, and everyone in town knows that you don't want him to leave, but I'm about to change all that. Once your little boy, Riley, gets laid, he ain't gonna want to hang around here any more."

Thelma leaned forward. "My God, you are such a slut."

"Your little boy will have glassy eyes and will be out of his head when I get done with him."

Just then, Riley entered the room, still drying his hair with a towel. "Clara," he said with a shocked look. "What are you doing here?"

Clara stood and walked over to Riley. She put her arms around him and gave him a passionate kiss that lasted for what seemed like a long time.

"I just stopped over to see if we are going out this Friday," she said with her arms still around him.

"Oh, yeah," he said with a smile. "Oh, yes. Oh, sure."

"Well, that's just great," she said leaning forward to kiss him again. "I'll see you then," she said then walked out the door.

"That woman is a whore," said Thelma.

Riley was still smiling as he watched her walk down the steps. "My God, I hope you're right," he said.

***

Belva walked into the kitchen to find Murphy still sitting at the table. Setting in front of him were two pieces of toast and a full cup of coffee.

"Is that the same coffee and toast I made for you over an hour ago?" she asked.

Murphy jumped and blinked his eyes. "What was that?"

"Never mind," she said. "I know damn well you ain't had a bite for breakfast. I swear you're going to waste away to nothing."

Murphy pushed the plate of toast away from him. "I'm just not hungry."

"Just what do you think the missus would say if she could see you now?" Belva asked.

"I guess she would be upset."

"You guess that she would be upset? Well, you guessed right. I don't mind telling you, Mr. Flemming, that you are going to do yourself some real damage if you don't eat right."

"I thought we talked about this Mr. Flemming stuff," said Murphy. "Actually, I thought you were going to call me Murph."

"I'm working on it," she said. "It's just going to take me some time to get used to doing something like that."

Murphy turned away and stared blankly at the wall.

"I worry about you, Mr. Flemming," she said with a soft voice.

Murphy blinked his eyes as if he was awakening from a sleep. "What did you say?"

"I said I'm worried about you. It's been too long since Katherine's death for you to still be mourning."

"And what makes you an expert on that subject?" asked Murphy.

"Don't you worry none about that, Mr. Flemming. I've been around, and I know when someone has crossed over the line."

"Crossed over what line?"

"It's the line between grievin' and gettin' on with your life kind of thing."

"And you would be an expert on the subject?"

"I actually know someone who is going through the same thing you are."

"Had this person lived with the same person for over a half century?" he asked with a sarcastic tone.

"My grandpa had been married to the same woman for sixty-two years, so to answer your question, yes, I have known such a person."

"Well, then, you must know that there are people who just don't want to go on living," said Murphy.

"Obviously, I didn't know Katherine as well as you did, but I knew her well enough to know that she wouldn't want you to be like this," said Belva. "It's my belief that she would have wanted you to be happy and get on with your life."

Murphy turned and stared out the window. "God, I miss that woman," he muttered.

It was about that time that there were footsteps on the front porch. Murphy turned to see the local marshal standing at his front door.

"Hey, Bud," said Murphy motioning with his hand. "Come on in."

Bud slowly opened the screen door and quietly stepped inside.

Murphy's smile disappeared. "You look as if you lost your best friend."

"Got some bad news for ya, Murph," he said looking at the floor. "Your granddaughter was in an accident."

Murphy jumped to his feet. "What?"

"She was riding her bicycle along the highway, and some woman hit her with her car," Bud said.

Murphy turned to Belva. "Did you know she was out riding her bike?"

"She never said a word to me," said Belva. "I thought she was out in the barn."

"Where is she now?" Murphy asked.

"They took her to Heartland."

Murphy turned to Belva. "Call her folks, and I'll call you later." He turned to Bud. "Thanks, Bud. I'm on my way to the hospital."

Heartland was only thirty minutes away, but it was the longest and most agonizing thirty minutes that Murphy had ever known. Not knowing her condition or even if she was alive was torture. He wished that he had taken Katherine's advice and bought a cell phone, but he knew without any doubt that nobody at Heartland would give information over the phone.

Murphy ran inside the front door and stopped at the front desk. He was politely told that she was in surgery and that he would have to go to the waiting room. Even though he had expected her to say that, Murphy was disappointed just the same.

It was a short time later that Murphy looked up to see Lloyd and Helen enter the room. They walked quickly across the room and stood in front of him.

"How is she?" asked Lloyd.

"I have no idea," said Murphy. "They told me she was in surgery."

"What happened?" Helen asked as she took a seat next to Murphy.

"All I know is that she went for a ride on her bike, and some woman hit her with her car."

"And I'll bet she was on her cellphone," said Lloyd.

Murphy paused as he studied his son and his wife. "I'm surprised to see you both here."

"This is our daughter, Dad," said Lloyd. "What did you expect?"

"I don't know," said Murphy. "I guess I was expecting you and your girlfriend."

"That was a cheap shot, Dad," Lloyd said.

"He says that he broke it off with her, Murphy," said Helen with a tone of sarcasm. "Of course, he wants me to believe that they never had sex either."

"When will you get it through your thick head that we were just friends?" Lloyd asked.

"When will you get it through your thick head that I'm not that naive?" Helen retorted.

"Alright, you two," said Murphy. "Let's not forget why we're here."

"Actually, there's no reason for you two to be here," said Murphy. "You know darn well that we won't get into see her for days, so why don't you guys go on home, and I'll call you when you're needed?"

"Oh, I can't ask you to stay here," said Lloyd.

"You're not asking me. Remember? I'm offering."

"You don't mind?"

"I have nothing on my plate," said Murphy. "Go ahead and get out of here."

They both slowly got to their feet.

"Are you sure?" Lloyd asked.

"Go on. Get out of here."

They started for the door when Helen stopped and turned to Murphy. "We have some matters to take care of, and then we'll be back. There's no way I can stay away, but thanks anyhow."

***

Heartland Community Hospital had been open for ten years before Murphy even knew it existed. Nestled in the small town of Sunbury, Heartland not only seemed isolated from the rest of the world, it seemed as if they wanted to remain private and secluded from anyone who might need medical help. In spite of its isolation, for some unknown reason, it attracted only the best doctors and nurses seeking employment. It had become the center of many discussions and debates as to why nearly every graduate of medical school began his search for employment at Heartland. Whatever the reasons, the end results were a medical facility in the middle of the farmlands with rooms available and some of the best medical people in the state.

It had been two days since the accident. Doctors at Heartland had worked round the clock trying their best to keep Emmy alive. There had been severe internal bleeding and respiratory problems brought on by the tires running over her chest. As if that wasn't enough, she suffered severe head trauma from being dragged down the road by the car. As everyone guessed that had been to the scene of the accident, the loss of blood suffered by Emmy was nearly enough to have killed her as well. One doctor estimated that if she had lain in that road for five more minutes, she would have died right there.

Murphy shifted his weight on the hard plastic chair. It was a small waiting room. With only ten chairs and two vending machines, there was very little room left for anything but sitting in a chair. Fortunately for Murphy, he was the only occupant at the time, which gave him room to stretch and pace the floor.

From time to time a doctor would stop by and give Murphy an update on Emmy's condition. He would try to present a positive outlook on Emmy's condition, but no matter how hard he tried to sound positive, it was clearly obvious that there was little hope of her recovery. Still Murphy persevered. It wasn't that he didn't trust the medical profession or that he didn't believe they were doing their best, he simply believed that good things resulted from positive thoughts, and in the final analysis, it was now all in God's hands.

As night began to fall and Murphy was coming to the end of the second day, a nurse stopped in. As always, Murphy jumped to his feet anticipating news of Emmy's condition.

"Good evening, Mr. Flemming," she said.

"Any news?" he asked.

"I'm sorry, Mr. Flemming, but nothing has changed."

Murphy sat back down and leaned back. "What can I do for you, then?"

"All of us here at Heartland are keenly aware of what you're going through. You've been here for two straight days now. Why don't you go home and get some rest?"

"I'm sorry," said Murphy. "But I must be as close to my granddaughter as I can. She needs me now more than ever."

"She is in a coma right now," said the nurse. "If anything changes, we will call you."

"You don't understand. I'm not just another one of your average run-of-the-mill grandfather. I lost one important person to me and I don't want to lose this one."

The nurse took a seat next to Murphy and gently placed a hand on his. "You haven't eaten in two days, have you?"

"How did you know that?" asked Murphy.

She pointed at the trashcan. "Every morning the janitor empties the trash. I asked him if there was anything from the vending machines in it. You can't keep going like this, Mr. Flemming."

"I'll be okay," he muttered.

"Besides all that, we know you haven't slept either."

"Well, that's where you're wrong. I've had frequent catnaps."

"That's not good enough," she said. "You need to maintain your strength so that you can take care of your granddaughter when she goes home."

Murphy paused then turned to face the nurse. "Only days ago, I lost a woman who had been with me for most of my life. That's not going to happen this time. No siree. I'm not losing this young girl. So whatever it is that you do, go do it, because I'm not leaving here."

The nurse lightly patted his hand and got to her feet. "Well, I have good news. You can visit your granddaughter for a few minutes."

Murphy jumped to his feet.

"Follow me," she said walking towards the door. Murphy fell in behind as she led him to a room at the end of a hall. She stopped at the door and cautioned him not to touch anything.

Murphy slowly walked into the room. He stopped at her bedside and looked down at the young girl.

Unfortunately, he was not prepared for what he saw. There were tubes seemingly running in and out of her whole body. Since her lungs were crushed, a small plastic box had been inserted into her throat and a tube from a machine essentially did the breathing for her.

Murphy trembled as he stared at this once beautiful and vibrant young girl lying in a nightmarish world of survival. How could something like this happen? It's a man's duty to protect his kin, and he had failed. She had put her trust in this man, her fate in his hands and he had let her down. Tears fell down his face, leaping to the floor. How could he go on with his life carrying the burden of guilt of what he had done?

The old man eased himself down on his knees beside the bed. He gently took her hand and held it between his.

"I'm so sorry, Emmy. It was my responsibility to protect you, and I failed you. I think you know I'd give my life for you, and, yet, this happens. Don't worry. Nothing like this will ever happen to you again. I'll see to it. Where ever this takes you, I will follow. I failed you once. It won't happen again."

It was an hour later that a nurse led him out of the room. As he approached the doorway, he stopped and stared at this young, helpless woman pitted against the mercies of the unknown. The guilt was almost too much to bear. He left the room a sadder man, a man with thoughts not only of her impending fate but his as well.

The third day came and went with little or no change. One doctor tried to instill a sense of hope by citing other cases where the victims had survived even worse injuries and had returned to their normal lives. Murphy wasn't impressed, since they had nothing to do with Emmy's condition. The doctor soon realized he was wasting his time and left the room.

Murphy's condition was worsening by the hour. His hair was greasy and unkempt, his face covered with gray stubble beard. The light that once sparkled from his bright blue eyes was gone now, replaced by worry and desperation. Kind and thoughtful nurses were now leaving food and water in the room. He had succumbed to drinking nearly all of the water, but as yet, only nibbled at the food.

Worry and concern for Murphy's condition spread throughout the hospital. What began as an act by a stubborn old man had now turned Murphy into a martyr in his own right. Over the years, many of the medical staff had witnessed acts of love, but nobody had ever seen anything like this. Murphy was slowly killing himself. He was nutritionally starved and exhausted beyond human endurance, yet he persisted.

News of what was happening had spread throughout the town of Springfield. Even those who barely even knew Murphy were at the very least concerned. There was small talk in every business and every street corner as to what action to take with no results.

Finally an impromptu meeting was held at the diner. As fate would have it, nearly all of the closest and most influential people in Murphy's life just happened to show up at the diner at the same time. What force brought them all together at that particular time has been debated ever since. In spite of everything, they all appeared within minutes of each other. A spirited round of discussion followed and soon, with hardly any debate, a plan was conceived. It was by no means sophisticated or involved. They simply decided to send some of Murphy's closest friends to see him. Being Murphy's best friend, Walter was unanimously chosen as the first to go.

By the fourth day, Murphy was so exhausted he could hardly stand. The night before, one of the nurses escorted Murphy to a vacant room to allow him to take a shower. Another nurse had brought Murphy clothes that had belonged to her husband. It felt good to Murphy to be clean again. He hadn't realized how miserable it could be to go that long without bathing.

It was early afternoon when the first of his visitors stopped by. Murphy was sitting in his chair staring at the wall when Walter walked through the door.

"Hey, Murphy," he said half-heartedly lifting one hand as if waving.

Murphy turned in his chair. He forced a smile. "Hi, Walter."

Walter walked across the room and took a seat next to Murphy. He frowned as he studied Murphy's face. "Jesus Christ, Murphy. You look like shit."

Murphy turned back around and faced the wall. "Coming from a horse's ass."

"No, really," said Walter. "What the hell happened to you?"

"If there's a purpose for your visit, Walter, get on with it."

"I just wanted to see how you were doing and to say hi."

"Somebody put you up to this, didn't they?"

"Why do you say that?"

"Because you're not that thoughtful," said Murphy. "Now who put you up to this?"

"What makes you think I'm not..."

"Who put you up to this, Walter?" he asked with a commanding voice.

"The whole town did, Murphy. Everyone is worried about you."

"And they sent you?"

"Why not?" asked Walter. "We're good friends and shit."

"Walter, these people are expecting you to have the perception and insight to report back to them on my condition. Half the time that I see you, you don't even zip up your pants."

Walter jumped a bit in his chair. "I don't see what that has to do with..."

"Never mind, Walter," said Murphy. "Just ask your questions and get out of here."

"Questions? Was I supposed to have some questions?"

"Do you have something to tell me?"

"Tell you? Oh, yeah. I finally got laid, Murphy. What do you think of that?"

"I really don't care to hear about you having sex with Agnes," said Murphy.

"Well, it really wasn't sex in the true sense of the word," said Walter. "You see, we..."

"Oh, God, Walter. I really don't want to hear any of this," said Murphy. "Thanks for coming over, but you've got to get out of here."

"Jeez, Murphy. I just got here. I really don't have much to tell the others."

"Go, Walter," said Murphy with a stern voice.

"Boy, you're not very friendly," said Walter.

Murphy turned and pointed a finger at his friend. "I have a granddaughter in the next room who's all but dead, Walter. What do you want from me?"

Walter's face grew sullen. He slowly got to his feet. "I'm sorry, Murphy. You're my best friend, and all I wanted to do was to take your mind off your problems even if it was for just one minute. I love ya, man, and I hope she pulls through."

Murphy ran his hand through his hair. "I'm sorry, Walter. I didn't mean to..."

"That's all right," said Walter as he shook Murphy's hand. "Take care of yourself, my friend."

It was nearly an hour later. Murphy was sitting in a chair staring at the wall when through the door walked

Belva. He was still unaware of her presence, so she took the time to study his condition. She was nearly appalled at what she saw. It was if he had aged decades in as little as a week.

"Murphy," she called out softly.

He turned blinking his eyes as if coming out of a trance. "Belva," he said struggling to his feet. "How nice to see you."

He gave her a quick salutatory hug, and they both sat down.

"How's Emmy, Murphy?" she asked turning her chair towards him.

"No change," he said. "She's still in a coma."

"I'm sorry, Murphy."

He nodded as acknowledgement.

"I thought Lloyd and Helen would be here," she said.

"They're here for a while and then they're gone. I guess there's more important things going on than their child's life."

"How are you doing, Murphy?" she asked. "You don't look good."

Murphy settled back in his chair and stared straight ahead. "Isn't it funny?" he blurted as if by himself.

"What's that, Murphy?"

"The term, old age, has such a benign sense about it. To most, it is a sweet phrase that brings up an image of a comfortable life free of child-rearing, financial burden, simply a time to rest and relax. I see it differently now. It's a portent of death. One day you look into a mirror, and there it is staring back at you. You examine your face and wonder what happened to you and when did this occur? There seems to be a distinct time in everyone's life when they cross over the threshold between youth and old age. It happens so subtly, almost as if the beast called old age has your number. He will stalk you from that point on, consuming you with each day. He has you in his clutches. The warm spring days of youth are gone now. A monster has you in his grip, and there is no escape.

It's like a playground slide that carries you into the abyss. You fear this beast you cannot see. You fear the ultimate destiny he has planned for you. We're all destined to go there. There is no escape. The strong, the weak, the smart and the challenged, we are all going there. There's no escape. Yes, I look into that mirror and see a man grotesquely altered from boy to man and from man to old age. I don't even recognize that old-age man. All I know is he will protect her this time. Her safety is in his hands, and if the beast pulls her into that abyss, I will follow. She's mine to protect no matter what."

Belva grabbed him by the arm. "Murphy...Murphy," she called out with a loud and stern voice.

Murphy jumped and lightly shook his head. "Oh, I'm sorry," he said. "I must have dozed off."

"Murphy, you need to get some rest," she said. "You're starting to lose it."

"No, I'll be okay."

"You're not even okay right now. You're close to having a serious problem."

"I know you mean well, but I'm not leaving."

"My, God, you are the stubbornest man..."

"You know, when Katherine died, I thought I would follow her to the grave. Katherine and I had been together for most of our lives. She was my partner, my mate and everything I could ever want. When she died, I wanted to go, too. I couldn't imagine a life without her.

Belva put her arm around his shoulders. "Murphy, I don't know about that kind of thing. What I do know is that medically speaking, you are in a serious condition right now. The lack of sleep, the stress, everything in your life right now is contributing to a situation whereby your body and mind are about to fail you, turn on you, simply give up. No matter how you put it, you are in mortal danger."

Murphy sat quietly not saying a word as he pondered what she had said. "Maybe it's time."

"Time for what?" she asked.

"Maybe it's time for geezers like me to move on."

"Do you mean to die?"

"Of course, that's what I mean," he said. "People my age have no useful purpose."

"I can't believe I'm hearing this," she said after staring at him in disbelief. "Let me put this in the most simplest of terms. You are killing yourself, Murphy, and you will die if you don't take care of yourself right now."

Belva wiped a tear from her eye. "You're wrong about one thing. You said you have no useful purpose."

"That's right," said Murphy without turning to her.

"Right now, there are hundreds of people in this town who are worried to death about you, Murphy," she said. "There are millions of people on this earth who will never know what it's like to be loved by so many. Most of us go through life and feel fortunate to have one good friend. Some are even luckier and have two, some even three friends, and here you are with a whole town at your side. My God, Murphy, most of the people in this town would do literally anything for you, and you have the nerve to refer to yourself as useless? I don't know what your definition of useful is, but I consider any man who has even one friend is not only contributing to this world but is serving God as well."

Belva started for the door then stopped. "By the way, Murphy, after you've killed yourself, and Emmy pulls through only to find that her grandfather is gone, what good did you do?" She paused for a moment hoping for an answer.

"Hey, Belva," he said without turning in her direction. "Thanks."

"You can thank me by going home to your bed," she said and walked out of the room.

It was nearly an hour later when a doctor stepped into the room. Murphy was asleep with his head leaning against the wall. He jerked forward when the doctor dragged a chair across the floor.

"Mr. Flemming, I just stopped in to see your granddaughter, and there appears to be no change," said the doctor. "It would seem that she is a tough girl."

Murphy rubbed his eyes with the palms of his hands. "What can I do for you, Doc?"

"Mr. Flemming, I've known you all my life," said the doctor. "In fact, you used to take me fishing when I was a kid."

"Then why do you still call me Mr. Flemming? What's wrong with Murphy?"

The doctor blushed. "Oh, I could never call you anything but Mr. Flemming. It would be like calling my dad by his first name."

Murphy leaned forward. "You didn't come in here to go down memory lane. What's on your mind?"

"You're in trouble, Mr. Flemming. If you don't get some sleep right away, you're going to be in here as a patient. I know we've tried everything to get you to go home, but we've got one ace up the sleeve. If you agree to go home and get a good night's sleep, when you come back the next day, we'll let you stay in your granddaughter's room."

Murphy smiled. "Do you mean all of the time?"

"That's exactly what I mean."

Murphy paused. "Will you call me if anything happens?"

"I promise that a nurse will be there nearly the entire night."

Murphy paused again. "It's a deal."

The doctor got to his feet. “And take a bath while you’re home,” he said waving his hand. “Good God.”

It had been days since Murphy had been home. He felt a great and sudden relief as he opened the door and closed it behind him. It was if all his troubles had been lifted from his shoulders. He slowly trudged into the living room and collapsed into an easy chair. Within seconds, he felt himself falling asleep. He snapped his head and sat up straight in the chair. He knew that if he allowed himself to fall asleep in that chair, he would be there for the rest of the night. He struggled to get to his feet then climbed the stairs to his bedroom. He had no idea where Belva was and didn’t care.

The next morning brought sunshine streaming in Murphy’s bedroom, but it had no effect on him. It was early afternoon before he finally opened his eyes. He glanced at the clock then jumped out of bed. Moments later he was dressed and was racing down the stairs.

“It’s one o’clock in the afternoon,” he said with an angered look. “Why didn’t you wake me?”

Belva was standing in front of the stove. “Sit down,” she said with a smile.

“No. I have to go to the hospital.”

“Sit down!” she demanded. “You‘re going to have some breakfast. Besides, I’ve already heard from the hospital.”

“You did? What did they say?”

“If I tell ya, will ya sit down?”

“Absolutely.”

Belva stopped what she was doing and turned to Murphy. “Your granddaughter is awake, hungry as hell and wanting to come home.”

“Thank God,” said Murphy with a smile. “All the more reason I should get over there.”

Belva set a plate of food on the table. “Just as soon as you eat.”

Murphy paused then smiled a broad smile. "Yeah…yeah, this is going to happen. I'm hungry."

Belva sat down across from Murphy. "Ain't seen that smile in quite some time."

"What did you expect?" Murphy asked as he sipped his coffee. "With Emmy in the hospital and everything."

"No, I'm talking about a long time before Emmy. I'm talking about a time before Katherine died."

Murphy's eyes went blank as he stared at a wall. "It's been a rough period in my life."

"I gotta tell you I was worried about you," she said. "I actually thought you might commit suicide."

"Well, there was a time…"

"And yet you're smilin' now," she said. "Why do you think that is?"

"That's pretty obvious," he said. "Emmy is going to be alright."

"You don't get it, do you?"

"What?"

"You're back," said Belva. "You've come back to the living. You care for Emmy. She means more to you than your own grief. You're back to the old Mr. Flemming who cares for others more than himself."

Murphy smiled and turned to Belva. "You know, I think you're right."

"Of course, I'm right," she said. "Was there ever any doubt?"

Murphy reached over and placed his hand on hers. "The best thing I ever did was to let you stay here."

Belva placed her other hand over his and smiled. "It worked out pretty good for me, too."

They smiled at one another for a moment, and then Belva got to her feet.

"You best be getting over to that hospital and see about that child," she said picking up his empty plate.

He jumped to his feet. “Oh, yeah,” he said starting for the door. “Hey, when you get a chance, would you call…”

“Already did,” she said without turning around. “Lloyd and his wife should already be there by now.”

Murphy started for the door. “Belva, you’re the greatest.”

It was a wonder that Murphy wasn’t pulled over for speeding. He arrived at Heartland in what seemed like half the time. He practically ran down the hallway until he came to Emmy’s room. When he reached her door, he slowed down and eased himself into the room. Both Lloyd and Helen turned to greet Murphy. They both wore smiles.

“Hi, Dad,” said Lloyd pointing at Emmy. “After we told this young lady what all you did, she has a new hero.”

Murphy slowly walked over to the side of her bed. She had tubes running in and out of her, but she was wearing a broad smile.

“Hi, Grandpa,” she said with a soft voice.

“Hi, Sweetheart. How are you feeling?”

She glanced down at the tubes running across her body. “Pretty good, all things considered.

“You had us scared there for a while,” said Murphy with a sense of relief.

“I’m so sorry for causing so much trouble.”

“Well, it wasn’t your fault,” said Murphy. “That woman ran off the road when she hit you.”

“I’m not talking about the accident,” said Emmy her smile disappearing. “I’m talking about before the accident when I was so disrespectful.”

“You’re a teenager,” said Murphy. “That’s what teenagers do.”

“There’s no excuse for acting like that,” she said. “I’m very sorry, and to you as well, Mom and Dad.”

"Emmy, I'm so happy that you've changed," said Lloyd. "But what happened for you to suddenly change your attitude?"

"I don't know. It must have been the accident. All I know is that I want another shot at life. I never thought I'd miss seeing the roses in bloom, playing around in Grandpa's barn or just watching it rain."

Murphy leaned closer. "Sounds like my Emmy has a new appreciation for life and now realizes how fragile it can be."

Emmy smiled. "Sorry, Grandpa."

## Chapter Twelve

It was a warm summer morning when Riley stopped in front of the bench. Walter and Sully were already there yelling and pointing fingers at each other. Riley paused as he watched them, trying to decide whether to stay or go back home.

"Morning, guys," he said as he got out of his truck.

Neither one responded but grew silent.

"I can see this is going to be a good day," said Riley as he took a seat across from the two men.

Walter pointed at Sully with his thumb. "Every day this guy has to prove he is a dumbass."

"You think Sully is a dumbass?" Riley asked. "What are the odds of that?"

"Walter is upset that I'm having sex with his ex-wife," said Sully.

"In the first place, Gladys doesn't believe in sex," said Walter leaning forward. "And in the second place, that would mean that you are not a homosexual, and we all know that's not true."

"That might not be true," said Riley. "I saw on the Doctor Phil show that there are guys out there that are straight *and* queer."

Walter paused for a moment. "Well, I guess it doubles the chances for a date on a Saturday night."

"Anybody heard from Murph?" Riley asked.

"Haven't heard squat," said Walter.

"Someone said that he finally went home from the hospital," said Sully.

It was about that time that the men looked up to see Murphy's truck stopping in front of them. He got out of his truck, and with a big smile and a wave of his hand, walked up to the benches.

Walter extended his hand. "Murphy, you old son-of-a-bitch, how are ya doing?"

Murphy took his hand. "Much better, my friend. And how are you guys?"

"We're the same old bunch," said Riley. "Just a little older and a lot crankier."

"How's your granddaughter?" Walter asked.

"She's going to be okay," said Murphy taking a seat next to Riley. "Run over by a car, and she's going to be fine. Can't get much tougher than that."

"We heard she was out of it for quite a while," said Riley.

"It was touch-and-go there for longer than I wanted."

Sully smiled. "Well, Murphy, you'll never know how glad I am to see you again. It's been hell dealing with these two horrid individuals, and having someone with a little class to talk to is an incredible relief."

"It's good for us having him back as well," said Walter. "At least we don't have to worry about him touching us inappropriately."

"Why would I touch you when I have your ex-wife to touch, and she doesn't call it inappropriate?" Sully asked with a smile.

Walter got to his feet and folded one of his hands into a fist and grabbed Sully with the other one. "Why, you son-of-a-bitch! I ought to…"

"Walter, sit down," said Murphy. "Now, what's this all about?"

Walter pointed a finger at Sully as he sat back down. "Sully, here, moved in with Gladys and has to rub it in my face that he's having sex with her. It's obvious that he is lying because she never did like sex, and dumbass here only has sex with guys."

"Hey, you had your chance with Gladys," said Sully with a broad grin. "It's not my fault you didn't know how to take care of her."

"What do you mean by that?"

"You know what I mean."

"No, I don't. I hope you're not talking about sex."

"Of course I'm talking about sex," said Sully. "You're no different than just about every other man out there. They have no idea how to give a woman an orgasm. Hell, most of them don't care. As long as he gets his, that's all that matters."

"And I suppose you know how to give a woman an orgasm."

Sully crossed his legs and leaned back with a look of pride. "Somebody just recently told me that she never knew real sex until she had me."

Walter shook a fist at Sully. "I swear to God, Sully…"

Murphy scrambled to his feet. "Walter, it must be nice having the house to yourself. You've wanted that for quite some time now."

"Yes…yes, that has been nice."

"Got peace and quiet?"

"Oh, my God, yes."

"So what are you complaining about? This is what you've been wanting," said Murphy.

Walter paused. "That's not the point. It's listening to this friggin' queer bait telling me about having sex with Gladys."

Riley cleared his throat. "Sounds to me like you still have feelings for Gladys."

"Oh, for Christ's sakes," said Walter. "I never heard such crap…"

"Go ahead and admit it, Walter," said Sully, leaning forward. "You still love Gladys."

"I don't…There's no way I…I could possibly still be in love with that woman," said Walter leaning back on the bench. He shook his head several times. "There's just no way."

Walter turned to Riley. "What about you? How are you and Clara getting along?"

Riley ran his hands through his hair. "We had a bit of a rough beginning, but things seem to be looking up."

Walter smiled. "Have you made a date to hold hands?"

"We have, in fact, made a date to have sex."

"Wow," said Walter. "Congratulations."

"You two have actually set a date to have sex?" Murphy asked.

"That we did."

"Well, all I can say is good luck."

"Why are you looking like that?" Riley asked. "What's the problem?"

"Setting a date to have sex," said Murphy. "That's the problem."

"Why? What's wrong with that?"

"People don't make a date for sex," said Murphy. "Sex just happens. You're alone, you start to fool around, and then one thing leads to another."

"What makes the difference as long as we have sex?"

"You're putting pressure on yourself."

"So?"

Murphy paused. "So, you're going to have problems if you set a date and time."

"What kind of problems?" Riley asked.

Walter leaned forward. "You're not going to get it up."

"Huh?"

"You're not going to get a hard on, numbnuts."

"That's impossible," said Riley. "I'm as horny as a two-peckered billy goat."

"Murphy's right," said Walter. "You're going to walk in there and the two of you will expect something to happen. It ain't natural, and at our age, it's tough enough without something working against us."

Riley turned away. "Ah, I can't believe…"

Walter laughed out loud. "I can't believe you're over sixty and still a virgin. You're not gay like ole Sully here?"

"What if I am, Walter?" said Riley with a touch of anger. "What are you going to do about it?"

"Well, for one thing, I won't bend over to pick up something," Walter said.

Riley stared at Walter for a moment. "No worry there, 'cause I'm sure you couldn't get it up."

"Why is it we're always talking about gays?" Murphy asked.

"Because we got one right here in front of us," said Walter, pointing at Sully.

"Okay, let me ask you guys a question," said Murphy. "For the most part, we can all recognize a gay guy when we see him. Right?"

The others muttered their agreements.

"They talk funny and walk like they are gliding along," said Murphy. "For the most part, they're easy to spot. Believe it or not, most of them are happy with their lives and wouldn't change a thing, and yet there are others who would give anything to be straight, have a wife and a family. Now, I ask you, what does that tell you?"

No one responded. Everyone could tell that Murphy was in a preaching mode and really wasn't interested in getting a response.

Murphy only paused for a moment and continued. "It tells me that these people really have no choice. They didn't just one day simply decide that they wanted to be gay. I believe that God made them that way."

Walter raised his hand as if he were in school. "I always heard that God hates queers."

"Look at the world around you," said Murphy. "Look at how much diversity there is. Look at people. They say there are no two people that are alike. You have fat people, skinny people, smart people and dumb ones. With all the different trees, animals, plants and people in the world, I would guess that God made gays purposely to add variety. Think about it. These people were like this from the day they were born. They grew up talking, walking and acting gay. They had no choice. They don't purposely act like gays so they can get their asses kicked by narrow-minded dullards. God made them that way, and if He did, I can't imagine He hates them or even disapproves of them."

"Hey, Murph, want me to get you a soap box to stand on?" Walter asked.

"Leave him alone," said Sully. "I agree with what he's saying."

"No shit," said Walter. "It's no surprise that you would agree with that line of thinking."

"I know," said Murphy. "I sound like I'm preaching, but I wish people would just leave them alone. Why can't people just take care of their own matters and leave others alone? Life's too short, and if that's the way they want to live their lives, it's none of our business."

"Wow, Murph," said Walter. "You're really on a roll."

"I guess that when you nearly lose someone close to you, it makes you think about life and how precious it is. I read in the paper about a guy driving down the street and another car coming at him. The driver got distracted for just an instant, ran the center line and in a second or two they're both dead."

There was silence for several moments, and then Sully got to his feet. "Guess I'll go home, and, as a retarded redneck would say, bang the old lady."

***

It was just before dark when Riley pulled up in front of the weatherworn house trailer. He stopped and studied it. He had only seen it once before, but for some reason it seemed to be leaning even further now. He got out of his truck and waded through the tall weeds. He slowly climbed the steps and knocked on the door.

"Hey, there, Riley, old boy," said Clara as she swung the door wide. "Come on in and sit a spell."

Riley hesitated then stepped inside. "I was a little worried about…"

"Oh, don't worry about this old place a-fallin' over," she said taking a seat on the sofa. "Hell, just last week, I had two guys over here at the same time, and nothing happened." She started to laugh. "Well, that's with the trailer and such. Believe you me, there was a lot that happened."

Riley stepped over to the couch. The space next to Clara was filled with cats. She swept her arm across the surface. "Get out of here," she shouted and the cats scattered in all directions. Riley slowly turned around and sat down.

"So, what's been going on with you?" she asked as she brushed cat hair from the sofa.

"Not much. How 'bout you?"

"Same old stuff," she said. "Hey, you don't happen to have something you could stick under that one end of the trailer, do ya?"

"Well, let me see if I…"

"How's that mother of yours?"

"She's doing just fine," he said. "Thanks for asking."

"Have you always lived with your mother?"

"Well, ah…yes, I have."

"Don't you find that a bit strange?"

"Oh, I suppose there are those who would think so. I don't know if…"

"Didn't you tell me once that you've never had sex?" Clara asked.

"Yes…I'm sorry to say."

"Why are you sorry?"

"Doesn't that make me out to be a loser?"

"Livin' with your mother and still a virgin…yeah, that might qualify," she said snapping her gum. "Ever see a naked woman?"

"I have a whole box of Playboys under…"

"No, no. I'm talking about a real naked woman," she said starting to squirm. "One that you can reach out and touch."

"Once my mother didn't know I was home and came walking out of the bathroom after taking a shower. I almost ran right into her."

Clara smiled and stood up next to the sofa. She reached out her hand and took his. "Come with me." She led Riley into the bedroom, and the two of them sat next to each other on the side of the bed.

Riley took a quick glance at the room. It was a double-sized bed and nearly filled the room from wall to wall. What little room that was left was filled with blankets, sheets and dirty clothes.

"Come on. Let's get naked," she said and started to unbutton her shirt.

"Whoa," said Riley. "Aren't we going to get into bed first? Isn't there foreplay involved here?"

"When you weigh as much as we do, it's much easier to shed the clothes sitting upright than it is while lying down," she said, pulling off her shirt. "Now, get naked."

Riley slowly unbuttoned his shirt while Clara nearly tore off her clothes. By the time Riley was taking off his pants, Clara was completely naked. Riley sat back down beside her, still wearing his underwear. He glanced over at her nude body. Each of her two breasts was pointing straight down and had slid over to her sides. He looked down at her crotch but could see nothing but one of her rolls of fat.

Clara turned and spread her arms. "Well, what do you think?"

"Oh, wow," he said with little or no feeling. "This is really great."

Clara glanced down at his underwear. "I don't see a whole lot going on down there."

Riley looked down and then turned back to her. "What did you expect?"

"Well, I was hoping to see that you had erected a tent."

"Huh?"

"A hard on. I was hoping to see that you had a hard on."

"Well, it wasn't exactly what I was expecting."

"What were you expecting?"

"I thought I could look down there and see…well, the business end."

"What made you think that?"

"When I look at a Playboy, I can see down there."

"Oh, for God's sakes. Those pictures are all touched up."

"Do you mean those girls have their stomachs hanging down like that?"

"Maybe not as far as mine, but, yeah, they have big stomachs. It's just those photographers really know how to hide them."

"Must take a gallon of ink."

Clara paused. Her face turned to an angered frown. "Are we going to do this or not?"

Riley glanced down at his lap. "Don't we need participation from him?"

Clara sighed. "You really don't know what you're doing, do you?"

"Not a clue."

"Haven't you ever watched a movie where there's a couple making love?"

"When stuff like that comes on, I have to change the channel because Mother doesn't like to see that kind of thing."

"Do you mean to tell me that you've never had sex with a woman and haven't even seen such a thing on television?"

"Kinda makes me a virgin and a half," said Riley.

Clara picked up her shirt and hurriedly put it on. "Go on, get dressed and get out of here," she snapped.

"Ah, come on, Clara," said Riley reaching for his shirt. "You said that you'd teach me and be my first."

"This is becoming too sick and twisted for me," she said as she finished getting dressed.

Riley put on his shirt. "I'll pay you money."

Clara paused. "Just when I thought it couldn't get any sicker, you tell me something like that."

"Be a buddy and help me out here."

"Get dressed and get out of here. I hope I never see you again."

Riley finished getting dressed and started for the door. As he walked across the floor, the house vibrated and then shifted even more. He slowly tiptoed out the door, got into his truck and drove away.

***

It was a glorious sunset as red and orange streaks lit up the sky. Murphy kicked the porch floor, sending the swing in a back-and-forth motion. It was the end of another day for him. The sun sinking below the horizon seemed a bit depressing to Murphy. It was almost like watching the end of a life and the horror of death as it slowly took over.

It seemed as if he had always been on that farm. He was reared there by his parents, left for a while and then returned after they had died. Sometimes he felt as if his life had been a waste. He did what was right. He raised a family, took care of his wife and went to church every Sunday. He did what every good husband and father should do, but it just didn't seem to be enough. When his time came to leave this earth, what would he be leaving behind that would show that he had been here? Writers leave the written word behind, construction workers, great and tall buildings. It just didn't seem right.

The front screen door opened, and Belva stepped out onto the porch. She smiled as she breathed in the evening air.

"Sure am a beautiful evening," she said as she stretched her arms above her head.

"That it is," said Murphy.

She turned to the swing. "Mind if I join ya?"

Murphy scooted over. "Not at all."

She sat down after Murphy stilled the swing, then they both kicked it in motion.

"Enjoying the night air, or is something wrong?" she asked.

"Why do you ask if something's wrong?"

"Is there?" she asked.

"Not really."

"Yes, there is. I can tell."

"How can you tell?"

"You grow quiet and you come out here to sit on the porch."

"I do this all the time?"

"Yes, you do," she replied. "Now what's the problem?"

"Oh, I don't know," said Murphy. "It's not really a problem. I guess I'm just feeling sorry for myself. There are so many people in the world who will be remembered and even go down in history. What will people remember me for? Absolutely nothing. Hell, six weeks after I'm gone, I sincerely doubt that anyone will even remember my name."

"You're feeling a bit down, aren't you?" Belva asked.

"I told you I was."

"What about your son and granddaughter?"

"Oh, they'll grieve for me for a short while and then go on about their business as if I never existed."

"No. That's not what I'm talking about," said Belva. "When I asked you what about your son and granddaughter, I was reminding you that you're leaving behind two wonderful people. Is there anything better than that?"

Murphy paused. "Yeah, I suppose you're right. It's just that when I was a young man, I always thought I would do something with my life. I would be remembered as someone who made a difference, someone who made a contribution to society. The years went by so fast. Seemed like I got caught up in life's challenges. Once you get started at raising and providing for a family, nothing else matters, and now that I'm at the end of my life, it all seems so pointless."

Belva dropped her feet to the floor and stopped the swing. "Murphy Flemming, shame on you," she said turning towards him.

"What?"

"Shame on you for the way you're acting right now," she said with a strong and loud voice. "In the first place, you ain't all that old. You keep talking about how you be at the end of your life. Good Lord, unless you got some sickness you ain't told me about, you're still a young man. Hell, I done looked up your age, and I've got 'cha by two years. So, I got a personal interest in you not being at the end of your life, 'cause that puts me way overdue. Seems to me if you want to make some kind of a contribution, you best be doing it. In other words, get off your dead ass and get to moving."

Murphy turned to Belva with a warm smile. "You know, I think of you as my best friend."

Belva blushed. "I guess this would be a good time to bring something else up."

"What's that?"

"Well, as you know, I've been here under your roof for quite a spell. I guess you could say that it's been much longer than I had planned."

"Katherine put you up to this, didn't she?"

"How did you know?"

"I figured as much when you came up to me with some story about needing a place to live for a while," said Murphy with a big smile.

"You let me move in anyway?"

"Of course, I did. Katherine always did know best."

"Well, like I said before, I've done been here for quite a spell and was wondering if I should be moving on?"

"Do you want to move on?" Murphy asked.

Belva paused. "Not really."

"Well, that's good, because I need you right here with me,"

Belva smiled and shifted her weight on the swing. "That makes me glad."

Murphy turned to her with a solemn look. "I love you, Belva," he said and took her hand in his.

Belva paused then smiled. "I love you, too."

## Chapter Thirteen

Riley pulled up to the curb and got out of his truck. Before he had even got seated, they were all asking about the previous night.

He waved his hands at the others. "Relax, guys. It was another disaster."

"Good Lord, what happened this time?" Murphy asked.

"Well, we got closer this time," said Riley. "In fact, we were nearly nude. At least, we got down to our underwear. She actually took off her bra."

"Did you see her boobs?" Walter asked.

"Yes, I saw them."

"Well?"

"Well, what?"

"What do you think?" Walter asked. "Did she have nice ones?"

"If snakes were boobs, she'd have a great set," said Riley with a disgusted look.

"What are you talking about?" Walter asked.

"They looked just like two snakes hanging from her chest," said Riley. "I didn't want to get too close for fear they'd bite me."

"I don't believe it," said Walter. "Look at how fat she is. Hell, that's the only good thing about fat women. They almost always have big tits. It kinda makes up for the rolls of fat you gotta look at."

Sully leaned forward. "Gladys has nice boobs. For her age, she has some real beauties."

Walter turned with an angered look. "I swear to God, if you don't stop that kind of talk…"

"All kidding aside, Walter, I need to ask you a serious question," said Sully, leaning even closer to Walter.

"I'm sure you'll admit that you have a certain amount of jealousy when it comes to Gladys."

Walter frowned. "I'm not jealous of that woman. No, sir. Not me."

"Well, then, why do you get so upset when I talk about having sex with her?"

"I don't get upset," said Walter.

"Walter, you just about hit me when I was talking about her boobs."

"Oh, I wasn't going to…"

"I think we all will agree that if jealousy exists, then there must be some feelings left inside you."

"What are you talking about?" Walter asked.

"I think you still love Gladys," said Sully.

"Oh, for God's sakes," said Walter. "There's no way that I…"

Murphy got to his feet. "Yes, you do, Walter. What Sully was saying is a fact. You wouldn't react like that when Sully talks about her. I would say that you have strong feelings for her. Besides, you just don't fall out of love with someone that you've been with for most of your life."

Walter leaned back and held up his hands. "Why are you guys ganging up on me?"

Riley stood up. "This is no joke, Walter. We're trying to help you."

"Well, why would you guys get involved in all this?

"Because we love ya, Walt," said Murphy. "We're all good friends or we wouldn't be coming down here every day. How much closer could four old geezers get than us?"

Walter stared blankly at Murphy. "I know you guys all mean well, but what makes the difference? Dumbass here is making love to her every day. Hell, he even lives with her."

Sully smiled. "No, I don't."

Walter whipped around. "What did you say?"

"I guess technically we live together, but we don't sleep together. In fact, we don't even sleep in the same room."

"Well, you might not be sleeping with her, but you've been having sex with her," said Walter.

"No, I haven't," said Sully.

"Well, yes, you have," said Walter. "You sat right there on that bench and told me all about it. I remember because it used to piss me off something awful."

"Oh, it pissed you off, did it?" said Sully, getting to his feet. "It pissed you off because you still have feelings for Gladys. Admit it, Walter. You still love the woman, or else you wouldn't get so upset with me."

"So, you haven't had sex with Gladys?" Walter asked.

"No, I haven't."

"Well, why did you make me think that you had?" Walter asked.

"I wanted you to find out for yourself how you actually feel for her," said Sully.

"Gladys put you up to this, didn't she?"

"No, this was my doing. She went along with it because I asked her to," said Sully. "Actually I think she was a bit curious to see if you had any feelings left for her."

Walter turned to the others. "Did you guys know about all this going on?"

"Yes, we knew all about it," said Murphy. "You got to understand. We didn't treat this as a joke. We want the best for you, my friend."

Riley nodded his head.

"I don't know whether to shake your hands or kick your asses," said Walter.

"Hell, you couldn't get your foot up that high anyhow," said Murphy.

"Well, what do I do now?" Walter asked.

"I'd say you need to take that up with Gladys," said Riley.

"You mean like going over to see her?" Walter asked.

"That would be a good idea," said Murphy, with a grin.

"I can't do it."

"Why not?" Murphy asked.

"I'm too nervous. I just can't do it."

"Well, that's something you'll have to work out with Gladys."

Sully smiled. "Here's the real question for you. Do you want me to stay with Gladys or come back to your place?"

"I can't believe I'm saying this but get your ass back home," said Walter. "I don't want you in the same house with Gladys."

A stillness fell on the group. They all leaned back as if something important had been resolved. Then, Walter's face grew sullen. He turned to the others.

"I can't believe you guys all plotted this thing against me and behind my back," he said with an angered voice.

In an effort to change the subject of conversation, Riley turned to Murphy. "How's your granddaughter doing?"

"She's doing great," said Murphy with a warm smile. "Her parents are taking her home real soon."

"Wait a second," said Riley. "I thought her parents had broken up."

"That's the only good thing that came out of this whole mess," said Murphy. "They seem to have mended fences and are getting back together again."

"That's great," said Riley. "That's really great."

A sad look spread across Murphy's face as he turned his blank stare to the ground in front of him. The others were aware and said nothing.

"Too bad Katherine didn't live to see that," he said wiping his eyes.

Riley scanned the sky over their heads. "Someone said we're getting rain today."

"Wouldn't hurt. That's for sure," said Walter.

Murphy got to his feet and started for his truck. "Gotta go. See you guys tomorrow."

***

It was early afternoon when Murphy closed the back door behind him. He started down the walk towards the garage. The forecast called for rain, and already dark clouds were being ushered in by westerly winds. Murphy had been thinking about going to see his granddaughter and had finally decided to do it.

As he turned the corner that led to the garage, Murphy heard a noise from inside the barn. He turned and entered through the open doorway stopping just inside the venerable old building.

His eyes quickly scanned the interior. He could find nothing that might have caused the noise until he noticed a swallow flapping her wings and jumping from beam to beam in the dusty rafters of the sagging old barn. She seemed to be upset about something. A barn owl sat in his stately perch several yards away undisturbed by the commotion.

Murphy glanced down at the area just below the swallow and noticed a round, gray object. He walked closer to find that it was a nest lying on the ground. Somehow, this carefully made, intricately designed nest had come dislodged from its home in the safety of the rafters of this seldom-used building.

As Murphy neared the fallen home, the mother swallow became increasingly agitated. She was now flying frantically in small circles landing on a beam for only a second and then would resume her desperate flight.

Murphy stopped only feet from the nest. He could see that it was lying on its side, and two small speckled eggs were lying only inches away on the straw-covered ground. Both appeared to be still intact and had, indeed, survived the fall.

The mother swallow was now screeching in protest to the invader who was standing much too close to her fallen family. The majestic, old owl opened his sleepy eyes to see what was creating this raucous noise in this, otherwise, peaceful dwelling.

Murphy stepped back in an effort to calm her fears. He knew that there was nothing he could do, and that any intervention from him would prove fatal. He retreated until he was standing in the dark shadows of one corner of the barn. The bird was quiet now. He could see her nervously standing on one of the high beams and then suddenly swoop down to the ground. He was not in a position where he could see her but decided to remain there quietly so as not to disturb her anymore.

Murphy studied the old building. Missing shingles from the roof allowed daylight to pour in and spotlight small patches of straw-covered ground throughout the barn. A few boards were missing on the backside of the building allowing even more light to penetrate the dusty interior. Several of the support beams sagged with the weight of all the years gone by.

Murphy glared out the dust covered, nearly opaque window. He remembered when the barn was new. It was a simpler time all those years ago. Young children screamed as one chased the other in circles around the feed storage bin in the center of the barn. Cattle that had been grazing in the north pasture all day leisurely strolled through the back door of the barn, somehow knowing that it was the time of day that feed was being poured into troughs.

Murphy breathed deeply. A barrage of smells and odors seemed to linger in his memory. Freshly-cut hay and recently-ground feed seemed to fill the air. Even the acrid and sometimes foul odors from the livestock seemed now to be a pleasant memory.

It was a warm summer day all those years ago. Murphy had just finished milking the cows and was about to feed the chickens when someone grabbed him from behind and screamed his name. His whole body jumped as a reaction and part of the milk that he was carrying spilled over the edges of the buckets.

Murphy whirled around to find his wife, Katherine, standing before him laughing hysterically. It seemed so strange at the time to see this woman who abhorred practical jokes standing there with her arms still outstretched. Suddenly, she turned and ran. Murphy dropped the two buckets of milk to the ground and gave pursuit. Still laughing loudly, she led him in a path that encircled the feed bin in the center of the barn.

The young woman had nearly run completely around the bin when Murphy caught her and pulled her to the ground. The two people embraced and rolled over several times in the fresh straw.

"I love you, Mr. Flemming," she said with a smile.

"I love you too, Mrs. Flemming, and you made me spill milk with that little stunt of yours."

"Try not to be so jumpy, Farmer Murphy," she said and rolled over on her back. They both stared up at the rafters of the barn while they caught their breath. "God, I love this barn," she said. "I feel so safe and comfortable when I'm in here. It's like no other place on earth. Do you understand what I mean, Murphy?"

"I suppose so," he muttered.

"No, you don't," she said. "You don't understand. You look at this place as storage for hay and a place to milk cows. To me, it's a special place. It's a sanctuary from the world."

"Whatever you say, Kat."

"Murphy, I want you to promise me something. I want you to promise me that if I should die before you that you will bury me in this barn. I want to spend an eternity in here."

"I'm not burying you in a barn," he replied. "Besides, there's no way that I'll outlast you anyway."

A gust of wind sent a whirlwind dancing across the floor of the barn. Murphy ran his hands through his hair and started for the open doorway. Suddenly, he felt a coldness seem to penetrate his body. He shuddered profusely. It was unlike anything he had ever experienced. For a moment, he could not move, and he found himself dropping to his knees, his arms frozen at his sides.

As quickly as it came, the coldness seemed to escape wildly from his body. The wind ceased, and a stillness fell on the barn and the surrounding area. Suddenly, a warmth poured over his body like sunshine in July. The warmness seemed to spread throughout his body and penetrate his very soul. His body gave a sudden jerk, and his arms slowly raised until they were straight out from his body. His eyes were closed, and his head tilted to one side.

"You're here, aren't you?" asked Murphy, his arms slowly lowering to his sides. "I can feel you once again." Murphy inhaled deeply, filling his lungs and then slowly exhaling. "I can smell you. I know you're here." Murphy opened his eyes and searched the barn. "I wish you could show yourself. I miss you so much. It's not fair, you know. It's not fair for you to leave me behind like that. I'm lost without you."

Murphy got to his feet and turned slowly searching the barn. "The kids are doing fine and so is Emmy. If it wasn't for Belva, I don't know what I would have done.

She's been a godsend to me, and we both know she's here because of you. I know it was you who had her ask me if she could stay here. I hope you'll understand when I tell you that I love that woman. Oh, it's not the kind of love you're thinking. It's the kind of love a friend has for another friend."

Murphy bowed his head. The warmth that had spread throughout his body quickly dissipated. He got to his feet and looked around the barn. Everything appeared normal again. The wind had subsided and a gentle rain began to fall. Murphy looked at the rafters overhead and could see that even the owl's eyes were once again closed, and he had returned to his daytime slumber.

He started for the doorway when he heard the soft chirping sound of a bird. He turned and slowly walked to the back of the barn. There, next to the fallen nest in the soft straw, was the mother swallow. She had, somehow, fashioned a nest from the loose hay and straw and was nestled over the two eggs that held her future offspring.

Murphy stared at the mother bird and marveled at her tenacity and dogged persistence in spite of the obstacles that life had thrown at her. Her home that she had painstakingly built for her new family had taken a disastrous fall, and yet, undaunted, she improvised and proceeded as if it were all a part of the plan. "Hey, little lady," he said aloud. "Life goes on no matter what happens, right?" A smile suddenly appeared across Murphy's face. He turned to the open space of the barn. "Thanks, Katherine. Life does go on, doesn't it?"

***

It was around two o'clock in the afternoon when Murphy got the phone call. Walter had been rushed to the hospital. It was thought that he had suffered a heart attack. Murphy jumped in his truck and sped off to the other side of town.

It was one of Murphy's worst nightmares coming true. He feared the worst and yet hoped for the best. Probably his best friend in the world was lying in a hospital bed, the minutes of his life ticking away, hoping for a miracle. It only figured. Here was a man who was on the verge of reuniting with his ex-wife and this had to happen. Why would God do this? Why do horrible things have to happen?

"Don't take him just yet, God," he muttered aloud. "He's a good man and deserves better. Sure he's a bit grumpy. We all are. It's just our way of having fun."

Murphy pulled into the hospital parking lot and rushed inside. He stopped at the desk and was surprised when they told him he could go right into Walter's room. He was expecting Walter to be in a critical condition and visitors not allowed.

"Hi, Walter," said Murphy as he approached his bed.

"Hi, Murph."

"If you needed someone to talk to, why didn't you call me?" asked Murphy stopping at his bedside.

Walter smiled. "Got tired of my own cooking. Must be pretty bad if I have to resort to hospital cooking."

"So, what are you doing here?"

"They tell me I had a mild heart attack. Scared the hell out of me."

"Are you going to be okay?"

"Oh, yeah," said Walter. "They want to do a few tests, and then I should be out of here later today."

"Sorry this had to happen," said Murphy.

"Sort of puts things in perspective if you get where I'm coming from," said Walter. "What once was so important becomes trivial when you think you're about to check out of here."

"Can we expect to see you tomorrow morning at the geezer bench?" Murphy asked.

"I don't know about that," said Walter. "But I'll be back there as soon as I possibly can."

"Pardon me for saying this, my friend, but you seem somehow different."

"You're darn right I'm different," said Walter with a smile. "I'm a changed man. That heart thing changed my life. No more am I the grumpy old geezer. I'm going to enjoy every day that I have left on this earth."

"I'll bet Sully will be glad to hear this," said Murphy.

"Sully is the first one I plan to apologize to. I can't believe how I treated one of my best friends."

"Wow! You are a changed man. I can't wait to see how Sully handles this."

It was about that time they both heard a gentle rapping on the open door. They both turned to see Gladys standing in the doorway.

"May I come in?" she asked with a soft voice.

"Gladys," said Walter with a broad and warm smile. "Please. Come on in."

Murphy slowly backed away. He held up his hand and waved good bye. "Take care, my friend."

Walter held out his hand as a sign that he wanted to embrace hers. "Gladys, what a pleasant surprise."

"I just had to come and see how you are doing after I heard," she said taking his hand in hers.

"How nice of you," he said. "I can't tell you how happy I am to see you."

"You are?"

"Yes, I am."

"Pardon me, but is this the same Walter I once knew?"

"The very same," he said. "Although you are looking at a new man. I want to apologize to you and every other person I've been mean to."

"Good Lord, Walter, I thought this heart attack was a mild one. What happened to you?"

"It made me realize how small-minded I've been. Life is too short to spend it as a grumpy old geezer. I'm going to enjoy life to its fullest. I figure from now on that every day is a gift from the Almighty upstairs."

"Well that's such good news," she said. "I guess the next thing I have to say should test your new attitude. Sully has moved back to your house."

"That's fantastic! I really want to make things right with that man, and having him back home is the best way to do it."

"Well, I wouldn't have believed it if I hadn't heard it with my own ears," she said.

"I know this is a little premature, but I'd love to take you out some night, after I get out of here, of course."

"I would love to go out with you," she replied with a smile.

"It's a date," said Walter. "I will call you just as soon as I get out of here."

"I'll be waiting."

# Chapter Fourteen

Over a week passed without Walter attending the morning meetings at the geezer bench. His health had improved enough for him to get around town, but he had decided to rest until he was confident that everything was okay. Sully was there for Walter, no matter what it was that he needed. In spite of their differences, he always considered Walter to be his best friend and had always said he would do anything for him. To the surprise of everyone including Sully, Walter remained in a good mood and a positive spirit. Not only was this a surprise to everyone who knew him, but was regarded as a miracle of spiritual dimensions. Walter not only became the most talked-about citizen in town but a model of positive attitude and a selfless concern for others.

It was nearly 10 o'clock in the morning. Riley and Murphy were already sitting on the bench when Merle Lingo, owner of the Lingo Dry Goods Store and owner of the benches, hobbled out of the store. He was an old man, slight in build and wore a perpetual frown. Unfortunately, he had a disposition that paralleled his frown and earned him many names from the townspeople that were less than complimentary.

"Well, good morning, Merle," said Murphy. "What brings you out of your cave on such a beautiful day?"

"Murphy, I want you and your buddies to stop sitting out here every day," he said.

Murphy paused as he stared at Merle. The smile disappeared from his face. "What did you just say?"

"The whole bunch of you gotta go," said Merle gesturing with his hands. "I don't want you and your pals sitting on my benches anymore."

"Why not?" Murphy asked.

"It doesn't look good. Besides, Molly over at the grocery store was complaining about you fellows."

"What was Molly griping about now?"

"She said she was walking by you guys the other day, and one of you farted," said Merle.

Murphy turned to Riley. "I remember that," said Murphy with a face full of laughter. As I recall very clearly, she was the one who farted. It was one of those kinds that dribbles out as you take steps. Christ, she was clear down to the bank and was still doing it."

"Damn! That thing stunk too," said Riley.

"Yeah. Do you remember that thing hung around for what seemed like hours," said Murphy.

"That's beside the point," said Merle. "I can't have you guys sitting out here. It just doesn't look good, and I won't tolerate complaints."

"Merle, were you listening just a moment ago?" Murphy asked. "Molly passed that gas, not one of us."

Merle started for the front door of his store. "You guys have to go."

Murphy turned to Riley. "Do you believe that?"

"Merle hasn't been himself since he lost Bernice," said Riley still watching Merle walk away.

"What are you talking about?" Murphy asked. "There was no question that Merle killed her somehow when he caught her in bed with Ben Higgins. We all figured she was in a freezer somewhere in the back of that store."

Just then a truck pulled up, and two men got out. Sully got out of the driver's seat and scampered around to the other side of the truck where he helped Walter step out.

"Well, look who's back," said Murphy as he shook Walter's hand.

"Nice to see you again," said Riley.

"You boys will never know how glad I am to be back," said Walter with a broad smile.

"Wow!" said Riley. "Would you look at that smile?"

"We had heard that your heart attack was life-changing for you," said Murphy.

"He's a new man," said Sully as he helped Walter sit down. "I'm still trying to decide which Walter I really like. I kind of miss the grumpy old version, but I will make a sacrifice and keep this one."

"Okay, Walter," said Riley with a hesitant voice. "How do you feel about what Sully just said about you?"

"Can't say enough good things about my old buddy here," said Walter patting Sully on the back.

"Good Lord!" said Riley. "This is the real deal. We should probably be introducing ourselves to you, because you're a stranger to us."

Walter settled into his seat. "So what's been going on around here? I feel like I've been gone for months."

"Well, on the positive side, Clara is going to give me one more chance," said Riley with a smile.

Walter reached into his pocket. "I came prepared for you, my friend." He pulled out a small blue pill and handed it to Riley. "You take this about an hour before you go over there, and you won't have to worry about getting a boner."

"Is this a Viagra?"

"It sure is, and wait until you try it. You could hang your coat on your thing after taking one of those."

Riley started to hand it back to Walter. "Oh, I don't think I should..."

"No, you don't. You keep that thing and use it. You ain't going to believe what that pill will do for you. That thing will be so hard you can chop wood with it."

"I hate to interrupt such a high-level discussion," said Murphy. "But we've got a problem. Before you guys got here, Merle came out and told Riley and me that we can't sit here anymore."

Sully and Walter both had a look of shock.

"Why would he say something like that?" Walter asked.

"Remember when Molly Pritchard walked by us a few months ago and farted?" Murphy asked.

"How could I forget?" said Walter. "I swear it was days before that thing finally cleared out."

"She's blaming it on us," said Murphy. "I really think old Merle is using it as an excuse for getting rid of us. Truth to tell, I think old Merle is jealous."

"Jealous," said Walter. "How do you figure?"

"All these years we've been sitting out here, we never once invited him, and I think it's made him a bit cranky."

"What should we do?" Sully asked.

Murphy sat up straight. "Well, I don't know about you guys, but I'll be here tomorrow morning and the morning after that."

"Don't worry," said Walter. "We'll be here. That will be the day when Merle Lingo scares me off. Besides, these benches might be his but they are resting on public territory."

Sully smiled. "I think even I could kick Merle's ass."

"I don't know," said Murphy. "That might be a close call."

"Murphy, I've been wanting to ask you a question for the longest time, but it's really none of my business," said Walter.

"Ask away," said Murphy. "I have nothing to hide."

"That Belva woman who came there to help Katherine. Is she still living with you?"

"That she is."

"It's a little surprising seeing as how Kat is gone now," said Walter.

"It's a long story, but she needed a place to stay, so I let her stay with me for a while."

"Well, if anybody gives you any shit because of it..."

"Shit about what?"

Walter cleared his throat. "You know...you and a black woman living together. You know how people talk."

Murphy took on a puzzled look. "Have there actually been people gossiping about Belva and me?"

"Well, Martha Rose from across the street was asking me about you and Belva," said Walter.

"The women down at the church were talking about you," said Riley.

"What are they saying?" Murphy asked.

Riley paused. "You got to remember that these are women talking to other women. They love to gossip."

"They're saying that Belva and I are having sex, aren't they?"

"Not in so many words," said Riley. "Women have a way of saying just enough words and with the perfect look on their faces to communicate with another woman. I don't know why they don't just come right out and say what's on their minds. I guess if they hint around like that, they figure they didn't really gossip about anybody."

Murphy got to his feet. "Gotta go, gentlemen. I have matters to attend to."

It was a long ride home for Murphy. He had been confronted with issues all his life. Some had easy solutions, others were a bit more difficult, but all could be resolved with common sense and appropriate action. This was different. This was an issue that Murphy had never faced before. His biggest fear was that Belva would hear the cruel and malicious things that the women in town had already begun to spread. Over the years, Murphy had known he was the target of gossip, but it was of no concern if it was directed at him. He only objected when it was an innocent victim such as Belva who fell into their sites.

Murphy stopped in front of the house to see Belva sitting on the front porch swing. He got out of his truck and started for the front door.

"Morning, Belva," he said stepping onto to the porch.

"Morning, Sir," she replied.

Murphy sat next to her. "You have got to stop calling me that. I don't even want you to call me Murphy. It's Murph to you."

Belva laughed. "For years, I'd work for these white folks, and I'd have to call them by mister so-and-so or missus so-and-so, and here you telling me to call you Murph."

"Well, look at it this way," said Murphy. "I'm not paying you to work for me, and you're not paying me to live here. The way I look at it, we're on equal grounds, buddies, friends. You're not working for a boss anymore. You are working with a friend."

Belva smiled. "That's one of the nicest things anybody ever told me."

"Well, you're a good friend of mine, and I wanted you to know that."

"I think of you as a good friend as well," she said.

Murphy paused. His face sobered. "There is one thing I think you should know. It might be a bit disturbing to you, but I think you should be aware of something."

The smile disappeared from Belva's face. "What's wrong? Is it something I did?"

"No, it's nothing that you did. It has to do with the narrow-minded citizens of our town."

"Oh, that," said Belva. "I can pretty much predict what you're about to say."

"What do you mean?"

"It's the women of the town and their gossip, isn't it?"

"As a matter of fact…"

"They're talking about you and me, aren't they?"

"Yes, that's exactly what they're talking about," said Murphy with a sober look. "I'm sorry that you must be dragged into such a mess."

"Sorry? Why be sorry? Hell, I'm flattered that they would even consider such a thing. There you are, such a handsome white man, and here I am, an old black woman. Sorry? Don't feel sorry for me."

"I am so relieved that you're not upset," said Murphy with a smile. "The women in our town can be so cruel."

"If they're talkin' bad about someone else, it makes them feel better about themselves."

"Yes, I suppose you're right," said Murphy, staring out across the cornfield.

"Murphy, do you mind if I ask you a question?"

"Sure. Go ahead."

"I've known you for quite some time now. It's not just me that you treat with respect but just about everyone you know. If you don't mind, would you mind telling me how you got that way? You see, not everyone is as kind as you are. Was it your parents who taught you right?"

"Oh, I'd have to say both of my parents were an influence, but my father especially," said Murphy.

"And why's that?"

"Pop had a heart as big as all outdoors, but you never knew it. He did things for people but would never let anyone know."

"Why was that?"

"I don't know. We never talked about some of the things he did. I'd hear about the kind and generous things he did from other people, but never from him."

"Why do you suppose he kept such things to himself?" Belva asked. "I would think he would have been proud."

"That's just the way he was. I'm guessing that it would have been too much like bragging."

"What kind of things did he do?'

"There were so many things he did that I never knew until after he died. Most of what he did were small things that meant a lot to others. I remember he'd collect soup can labels all year long, then in the fall when the leaves were changing, he'd drive down to a school in Kentucky to drop them off. I guess there was some program where schools could redeem them for cash. If there was a bad snowstorm in the winter, Pop would get up early on a Sunday and go around to the churches to shovel snow off the sidewalks and steps leading up to the main entrances. Most of the times he did that, it was so early nobody ever knew that it was Pop who did it."

"Sounds like he was quite a fella," said Belva.

"I have a favorite memory of my dad," said Murphy staring across the farmlands. "There was a very poor man who lived in a one-room shack down by the river. Everyone in town loved the man and respected him, but no one would do anything to help him. From what I heard, he had been a teacher in town and was admired by just about everyone. I guess he was crippled and couldn't leave his shack for anything. Pop would sneak down there about twice a week and drop off bags of food onto his doorstep. I swear if it hadn't been for him, that old man would have died from starvation."

"How did you find out?"

"It took a while, but I finally noticed him leaving the house ever so often at an incredibly early hour. It was long before daybreak, so I followed him one morning and watched him secretly set two bags of food on that man's porch. I never told Pop that I knew what he was doing, and you know what? He never told me or anybody else for that matter."

Belva bowed her head. "I never met your father."

Murphy paused. "There's not a day goes by that I don't miss him," he muttered.

In a few moments, Murphy kicked the floor and started the swing. They both leaned back and stared at the open field. After a short while, the swing came to a stop. Murphy gripped the front edge as if he were about to stand up. Belva slipped her hand softly over his. Murphy turned to find a warm smile on her face. He smiled back and gently took her hand in his.

***

Riley quietly opened the front door and stepped inside. He gently closed the door and tiptoed across the living room.

"Riley, is that you?" came a voice from down the hall.

"Yes, Mother."

"I'm in my bedroom. I want you to come here."

"You're in your bedroom? Imagine that," he muttered."

"What did you say?"

"Nothing, Mother."

He cautiously stepped inside her room.

Thelma sniffed the air. "My God, what's that smell?"

"I don't know," said Riley sniffing as well. "What's it smell like?"

"It smells like some cheap whore."

"Oh, that's probably my new cologne."

Thelma sat up in her bed and leaned forward. "What the hell did you do to your hair?"

Riley's eyes glanced up then returned to her. "I got it cut."

"That's a pretty fancy haircut for someone who doesn't have any hair."

"Okay, Mother. What did you want?"

Thelma paused as she studied Riley. "You're going out with that slut again, aren't you?"

"If you're talking about Clara Butts, yes, I am."

"I can't believe you're still seeing that tramp," she said covering her mouth with her hand. "She has to be the trashiest female in town."

"That's not a very nice thing to say," said Riley. "You couldn't possibly know her that well, considering how little you get out of this house."

"One look at her and you know she's a whore. Why any man would want to have sex with that fat pig is beyond me." Thelma paused as she stared at Riley. "That's what you're up to, isn't it? You're having sex with Clara Butts, aren't you?"

"Well…no…not really."

"What the hell does that mean?"

"I haven't had sex with her yet, but I'm trying my best to make it happen."

Thelma grabbed her head with both hands. "Oh, my dear God. I don't believe it! Where in the world did I go wrong?"

"Mother, once again, I must remind you that I'm over sixty years of age and have not been laid. I'd like to experience that pleasure just once before I die. Am I asking too much here?"

Thelma fell backwards into her bed rubbing her scalp. "Oh, please God, tell me this isn't happening."

"Mother, you're making a big thing out of nothing."

"A big thing out of nothing? You're going to have sex with some filthy whore who probably has all kinds of diseases, and you think that's nothing?"

"You're right," said Riley with a smile. "It will be something! It will be something I will cherish and remember the rest of my life!"

"Oh, dear God, help me," said Thelma, as she rolled over to face the wall.

# Chapter Fifteen

The next morning, Murphy parked his truck in front of the Merle Lingo Dry Goods Store and was shocked at what he saw. Riley was standing on the sidewalk with his arms spread wide. Murphy looked from one end of the sidewalk to the other and could not see the benches.

He got out of his truck and walked towards Riley. "What the hell happened to the benches?"

"My guess is that Merle wasn't kidding."

"He can't do that?"

"Well, I think those benches were the property of the dry goods store."

Murphy turned and started for the back of his truck. He leaned over the side and pulled out folding chairs. "I kinda figured old Merle would do something like this, so I came prepared."

The two men erected the chairs over the same spot where the benches once were then sat down.

"I should have known that old turd would do something like this," said Riley.

"Well, I've known that old turd all my life, and I pretty much expected it. That's why I brought along four chairs just in case."

"I still don't believe that he is doing this. How long have there been geezers out here?"

"As far back as I can remember," said Murphy. "It goes back before Merle even owned this place."

A truck pulled up, and two men got out. Walter stared in disbelief.

"What the hell happened here?" Walter asked.

"Your old buddy, Merle, is sending us a message."

"Well, I'll be," said Walter. "He's about to get his ass kicked."

"And I suppose you have someone in mind to do it," said Sully.

Walter sat down and sighed. "Why, me, of course."

Murphy stared at Walter. "Are you okay, my friend?"

"Oh, I'm fine. Just a little tired."

"Yeah, right," muttered Sully.

Murphy glanced at Sully then back to Walter. "Come on, Walt. I've known you for too long. Something's wrong."

"Not a thing. I'm fine."

Murphy turned to Sully. "Okay, Sully. What's wrong with him?"

"I'm staying out of this," said Sully. "He's a stubborn old shit, and I don't want anything to do with him."

"Let's change the subject," said Walter. "Who brought the chairs?"

Murphy paused. "I did."

"Kinda figured on Merle being a shit, huh?"

"One thing about Merle," said Murphy. "He means what he says, and if he says we gotta go, he will make that happen."

The front door of the dry goods store opened and closed, and an old man walked down the steps.

"I thought I told you old bastards that I didn't want you out here anymore," said Merle.

"You said you didn't want us sitting on your benches," said Murphy. "So we brought our own chairs."

"I don't want you out here at all. Take those fold-up chairs and get out of here."

Murphy smiled. "I don't know how to tell you this, but we're sitting on public property. Those benches might have been yours, but this sidewalk is for the public."

"By God, if that's the case, then I'm calling the marshal."

"Merle, what is your problem?" Murphy asked. "We've been sitting out here for years. We don't make any trouble. In fact, we talk people into shopping in your store."

"For one thing, you're blocking the sidewalk."

"Well, now, you know that isn't true," said Murphy. "Even Bertha Tubbs passes by us every day, and they don't get any bigger than her."

"Doesn't matter one bit. I want you guys out of here."

"It's because we have never invited you out here, isn't it?" Murphy asked.

Merle paused still maintaining his spiteful look. "Ahhhh…"

"Well, here's our formal invitation. Merle Lingo, would you be kind enough to join us as we sit in front of your store and yak about nothing?"

Merle put his hands on his hips then pointed at each man. "I'll get you bastards out of here if it's the last thing I do," he barked then turned around and walked back into his store.

"Good Lord, what crawled up his ass?" Walter asked.

"Merle gets into one of his moods every once in a while," said Murphy. "He'll come around."

"Maybe we should move," said Sully. "There's plenty of room in front of the library."

"No," said Murphy. "Tradition has it that we have always been right here, and we aren't moving because one old man is in a snit about something."

"Sounds good to me," said Riley.

Murphy smiled. "Riley, don't you have another date with Clara?"

"That would be tonight. I'm going over to her place and watch television."

"I thought you and her were trying to have sex," said Murphy.

"We gave up on that. We decided to try another approach. It just seemed as if we were rushing into things."

Murphy turned to Walter. "So tell me, Walter. What's going on in your life?" And don't blow me off, because we all know something is strange about you."

"Oh, things couldn't be better," said Walter. "In fact, I was thinking about inviting Gladys out on a date. The little trick that Sully played on me kinda opened my eyes."

"So you might have feelings for her after all?" Murphy asked.

"Hey, you just never know," said Walter, leaning back in his chair.

"What about you, Sully? Murphy asked. "What's been going on in your life?"

"Oh, nothing much."

"Still buying lottery tickets?"

"Today is the last day," said Sully. "The state has bled enough money out of me. If I don't become a millionaire today, it will never happen."

"Well, good luck," said Rilcy.

"What about you, Murphy?" Walter asked. "What's going on between you and that Belva?"

"That Belva? That Belva? You make her sound like some kind of animal."

"Whoa," said Walter. "Sorry. Didn't mean anything by it."

Riley leaned forward. "If I didn't know any better, I'd say you were defending your friend Belva."

"Well, sure I am. She's a human being, just like the rest of us."

All three men smiled and leaned closer.

"No, she's more than just another human being," said Riley. "It's obvious that you have feelings for this woman."

"So, what? What if I do? It has nothing to do with anybody else."

"Hold on there," said Riley. "We're all on your side. We're happy for you. We just want to know if you're aware of what's going on?"

Murphy got to his feet. "I might not have known a few minutes ago, but I know now. Gotta go, fellas. Take care."

In spite of his speed, the ride home seemed to take forever for Murphy. He pulled in front of the house and nearly jumped out of the truck. He opened the backdoor and found Belva sitting at the table with a cup of coffee.

Murphy spread his arms open and smiled. "Belva, let's you and I go on a date."

Belva stared at Murphy with her mouth open. "What did you say?"

"I asked you if you would like to go on a date with me."

"Are you kidding me?"

"No, I'm not kidding."

"Well, what brought this on?" she asked with a stunned look.

Murphy sat down across from her. "Are you going to deny that you have feelings for me?"

Belva leaned back in her chair. "Well, no. I guess not."

Murphy sat up straight. "I can tell you without any hesitation that I have feelings for you, so why don't we go out on a date?"

"Good Lord, I can think of a hundred reasons why we shouldn't," she said sipping her coffee.

"Does this have anything to do with the townspeople?"

"Yes. A good part of it does."

"What do you care what they think?"

Belva slowly shook her head. “Murphy, you have no idea what you’re getting into. These seemingly nice, quiet neighbors of yours can turn into absolute monsters. You’ll see a side of them you never thought possible.”

“I think you underestimate the people of this town,” said Murphy, the smile disappearing from his face.

“Oh, quite the contrary, Murphy,” she said. “I think you underestimate the people of this town. I’m an old black woman. The only way white people will put up with an old black woman is if she’s cooking, cleaning or singing to them, and there had better be a leash around her neck that’s held onto by a white person.”

“Belva, things have changed,” said Murphy. “White people are not that mean anymore. I’d like to think those days are over. Oh, there’s no doubt we’d get some looks. In fact, I’m not saying we would be the talk of the town, but you just cannot run your life based on what others think. Life is short, Belva. You gotta do what’s best for you, and the hell with what others think. Besides, I’ll be right there beside you. No one will hurt you.”

Belva stood and set her coffee cup in the sink. She slowly walked around to the other side of the table where Murphy had stood as well.

“You sure make a convincing argument, Mr. Flemming,” she said with a warm smile.

“So does that mean you’ll go out with me?” he asked.

Belva opened her arms. “I accept your invitation.”

Murphy wrapped his arms around her. “Thank you. You won’t regret it.”

***

Riley carefully walked up the steps to the trailer and rang the doorbell. Clara opened the door and swung it wide.

“Hey, there, Riley. How’s it hanging?” she said turning back inside.

"Doing good," he said stepping inside and closing the door behind him. He scanned the living room to find that she had cleared a path to the sofa and basically had piled the stuff in the doorway to the bedroom.

"Expecting company?" he asked.

"I'm expecting an overweight, over-aged turd who just happens to be a friend of mine.

"Well, until that turd shows up, will I do?"

"You most certainly will," she said opening the stove. "Hope you're hungry."

"I'm starved," he said picking up the remote control. "What are we watching on TV?"

"Find something, and I'll bring dinner."

Riley flipped through the channels and stopped at the news.

Clara brought a tray of food with steam billowing from it and sat it in his lap. "That's a brand new frozen dinner they just came out with," she said grabbing another tray and sitting down beside him. "Hope you don't mind, but I ain't much of a cook. At least I can grasp the concept of frozen dinners."

"Oh, I live on the things," said Riley. "Mother fixes a few of my meals, but I usually have my nose buried in the freezer, picking one out."

"Hope you like meatloaf."

"It's my favorite."

In spite of the exceptionally hot food, they finished in minutes, leaned back and patted their stomachs.

"Damn, that was good," said Clara.

"I'll never get tired of meatloaf," said Riley struggling to get to his feet.

"Where are you going?" she asked.

Riley stopped the struggle. "I thought I'd take our empty trays out to the kitchen."

"Why bother?" she said and tossed her tray onto the floor. Silverware and remaining food splattered across the carpet and onto the paneled wall.

Riley watched with a blank face. He held his tray out in front of him. "Well, I don't know whether I should…"

"Go ahead," she said gesturing with her hand. "You might have noticed I'm not what you call a neat freak."

Riley leaned over as much as he could and dropped the tray on the floor. "There we go," he said leaning back in the sofa.

"I guess there are those who might call you one," said Clara.

Riley turned slightly to face her. "My mother calls me a slob, but I don't think…"

Suddenly, Clara grabbed his cheeks with both hands and kissed his lips long and hard. Riley pulled back and stared into her face with wide open eyes. He paused then kissed her back with passion. He pulled back again, this time with short, panting breaths.

"How fast can you get out of those clothes?" he asked then kissed her once again.

"Faster than you can," she said pulling off her shirt. "Let me show you my bedroom, if you don't mind."

"I would be most grateful," he said as he nearly jumped off the sofa.

# Chapter Sixteen

The next morning, Murphy turned the corner and parked in front of the Lingo's Dry Goods Store. He looked up to see Riley smiling as he sat on the recently restored benches.

"Well, I'll be," said Murphy as he got out of his truck. "I don't believe it. Merle brought the benches back out."

"Is he going through some mid-life crisis?" Riley asked. "Yesterday, I thought he was going to take a gun to us, and now today, we're back in business."

"I have no idea what's going on," said Murphy taking a seat.

"Hopefully, Merle will join us after awhile and let us know," said Riley.

Murphy leaned back. "Pretty day, isn't it?"

"Pretty day? Yes, it's a pretty day!" Riley shouted with a broad smile. "Best day of my life! It just doesn't get any prettier than this day!"

Murphy paused. "You got laid last night, didn't you?"

"Yes, by God! I got laid! I had sex! I did the dirty deed! Life is good!"

"Wow!" said Murphy. "Was Clara that good?"

"How the hell would I know? What the hell would I compare her to? All I know is that I am finally not a virgin. I am a man of the world. I have had sex!"

Murphy smiled. "Well, congratulations. I'm happy for you. Are you going over to her place again?"

"Shit, I might move in with her," said Riley. "For the first time in my life, I think I'm in love."

"You might want to wait a while before you…"

"I ain't waiting for shit!" said Riley with a broad grin. "I plan to be there whenever that woman feels like having sex. She feels like having sex, old Riley will be there to take care of her."

Just then a familiar truck parked across the street.

"Looks like Walter and Sully are here," said Murphy.

"I can't wait to tell Walter," said Riley. "That son-of-a-bitch has been teasing me long enough."

Sully got out of the truck and started across the street.

"There's a new one," said Murphy. "I've never seen Sully drive the truck before."

"More importantly, where's Walter?" Riley asked.

Sully stepped upon the sidewalk and sat on one of the benches. "Morning, guys," he said with a sober face.

Murphy leaned forward. "Where's Walter?"

Sully stretched, looked away, then turned to the two men sitting across from him. "Walter is dead."

Neither Murphy nor Riley moved. They were frozen in the same spot as they replayed in their minds what Sully had just said.

Finally, Murphy slightly shook his head as if waking from a sleep. "What did you say?"

Sully wiped a tear from his eye. "Walter died last night from cancer."

"Cancer!" said Riley. "How long had he had cancer?"

"We're not sure," said Sully. "Remember when he had that heart attack? When he was in the hospital, they did some tests on him and found out that he only had days to live."

"Why didn't he tell us?" Murphy asked.

"I don't really know," said Sully. "But he told me not to tell. My guess is he didn't want things to change here on the geezer bench."

"Good God, I don't believe it," said Riley.

"The funny thing is I scratched off my very last lottery ticket, and I won," said Sully. "Unfortunately, Walter was already gone."

A silence fell on the three men as they thought about their lost friend.

"Is there going to be a funeral?" Riley asked.

"No, there isn't," said Sully. "He wanted to be cremated and his ashes spread up and down Main Street."

"Well, that seems fitting," said Murphy. "At least, he will still be around."

Silence fell again.

"Well, who are we going to get to replace him here on the geezer bench?" Riley asked.

"Oh, my goodness," said Sully. "The man isn't even cold yet, and you want to talk about his replacement?"

Riley jumped back. "Well…I guess maybe you're right."

The three men said nothing. Riley kicked stones on the pavement beneath them while Murphy rubbed his hands.

"Charlie Barth might make a good candidate," said Riley.

"I don't think so," said Murphy. "Remember? He voted for Carter back in the day."

"What about Warren Hedges?" Sully asked.

Murphy nodded his head. "He might be a good one."

32062115R00117

Made in the USA
Charleston, SC
07 August 2014